"So you think sex is disgusting."

Max observed Sarah with cold, clinical interest. "Is that what was wrong with your marriage?"

She rounded on him fiercely. "That's none of your business! Is a woman not a woman simply because she doesn't appreciate your overblown attractions?"

"Overblown?" His thin smile held a glitter of real annoyance. "How Victorian. Although you admit they exist. Coming from a woman who's so afraid of her own femininity that she deliberately desexes herself, I must take that as a compliment."

The remark, with its grain of unarguable truth, flicked Sarah on the raw.

"And I should be complimented by *your* offer of clothes? I'm impressed that you get as much pleasure from dressing women as you do from undressing them!"

Books by Susan Napier

HARLEQUIN ROMANCE
2711—LOVE IN THE VALLEY
2723—SWEET VIXEN

These books may be available at your local bookseller.

Don't miss any of our special offers. Write to us at the
following address for information on our newest releases.

Harlequin Reader Service
P.O. Box 52040, Phoenix, AZ 85072-2040
Canadian address: P.O. Box 2800, Postal Station A,
5170 Yonge St., Willowdale, Ont. M2N 6J3

Sweet Vixen

Susan Napier

Harlequin Books

TORONTO • NEW YORK • LONDON
AMSTERDAM • PARIS • SYDNEY • HAMBURG
STOCKHOLM • ATHENS • TOKYO • MILAN

Original hardcover edition published in 1983
by Mills & Boon Limited

ISBN 0-373-02723-0

Harlequin Romance first edition October 1985

CHAPTER ONE

'COME on, Sarah, get a move on! The plane was due in fifteen minutes ago.' Julie Somerville gave her assistant a harried look over the top of her typewriter.

'Don't panic, it'll only take me twenty minutes to get out there. They won't even have got through Customs. You know how notorious Auckland airport is at processing jumbos,' Sarah Carter replied calmly from the opposite desk.

She hated being rushed. To rush was to risk being unprepared and in her job that was tantamount to a crime. As editorial assistant on the monthly fashion magazine *Rags & Riches* she was constantly meeting new people —writers, models, advertising executives—and all expected her to know instantly what they wanted and why, and what Sarah was supposed to be doing about it. Usually she did, thanks to the overstuffed green filing cabinet squatting within arm's reach of her chair.

'Don't say "don't panic" in that maddening way, I think I've earned a good panic!' Julie declared. 'While you've been lolling about the city's beaches for three weeks I've been working at shriek pitch. Not only running this mad-house, but also trying to fend off the rumours that Wilde Publications has bought us out with the aim of rationalising their Australasian operations . . . by dumping *Rags*.'

'Well, from today you'll be able to let them do the fending,' Sarah soothed.

'If they don't spend their whole visit stranded at the airport, yes.' Julie jabbed viciously at the keys of her machine. 'I had everything nicely laid on for Thursday. This is going to completely derail my timetable. I nearly had a nervous breakdown when Janey brought in that telex first thing this morning. Damn!' The dark blonde head bent as Julie back-spaced and X-ed out an error in her copy.

Sarah grinned. Julie's nerves were an in-house joke, never in danger of being bent, let alone broken. She loved it when things went awry and she was called on to extract order from chaos, completely confident of her abilities. She was a good journalist and an excellent editor; ambitious, hard-headed, yet possessed of all the elegant femininity expected of a woman who edited a fashion magazine.

'Stop grinning and start moving.' Julie looked up again as she heard the rumble of a filing cabinet drawer. 'What are you up to *now*?'

'Looking for the file on Wilde's. I'd better know who I'm supposed to be meeting.'

'It's not there—I've got it. Anyway you haven't got time. Indulge your fetish for facts later, all you're doing is greeting them, not entering *Mastermind*! Max Wilde you *must* know, Tom Forest is a fellow director—financial expert.'

'But—'

'Oh my God!' Julie sat suddenly upright in her swivel chair, china-blue eyes focussing properly on Sarah for the first time.

'What's the matter?' The crack in the clear soprano voice was unnerving.

'Grape! You had to wear the dreaded Grape, on today of all days.'

Sarah looked down at her dress, a short-sleeved shirt-waister with a matching belt. It had been the first thing to hand in her wardrobe, so she had put it on.

'I had vain hopes you might have done some shopping during your holiday.' Julie rolled her eyes. 'What kind of impression do you thing the Grape is going to make? If only I didn't have this meeting . . . what's the weather like outside?'

'I am not wearing a coat. Not in Auckland. In February,' said Sarah firmly.

'This is the son and heir of a world-famous couturier we're trying to impress here,' Julie wailed. 'He'll be expecting style . . . panache . . .'

'He'll be expecting you,' came the mild reply. 'And we can't all look as good as you do.'

Julie was in her late thirties but with her rippling shoulder-length blonde hair, glowing, peachy skin and lithe figure she could have been ten years younger.

'You don't even try, Sarah. Why don't you—'

The phone on Sarah's desk rang and she snatched it up. Once Julie started on the subject of clothes she could go on for hours.

'It's Keith.' She hugged the receiver to her chest. 'He wants to know if the panic's still on and whether you want to see the paste-ups now?' Keith Moore was their art director. It was the triumvirate of him, Julie, and photographer Mike Stone who were responsible for creating *Rags*' distinctive, successful, identity.

'Yes and yes. I may as well see them, I seem to be suffering from terminal writer's block here.' She tore the paper out of her typewriter and screwed it up in disgust.

'What paste-ups?' asked Sarah, replacing the receiver.

'We've done a mock-up of the April issue,' Julie explained. 'New ideas for new publishers. We were going to get a dummy printed, but we won't have time now.'

'Isn't that assuming rather a lot? Wilde's may not want to make any changes.'

'We're a little on the staid side, sweetie, you must admit and Wilde Publications isn't noted for its conservatism —nor is Max Wilde. Since I don't think he's coming all this way just for his health it stands to reason he has plans. There's a memo of mine about it somewhere—Janey, don't you ever *walk* into a room?'

'Sorry.' Julie's young, freckle-faced secretary looked anxiously at Sarah. 'I just rang to check for you about whether the flight from London was on time. It wasn't.'

'There, I told you not to panic, Julie. How late is it?'

'Not late,' yelped Janey. 'Half an hour early! Tailwinds or something.' Her voice rose to follow the blur that was Sarah.

So much for not rushing. Fleeing for the stairs, Sarah cursed the fact that they were on the fourth floor of an old building. There were only two lifts and they always seemed to be rattling up when you wanted to go down.

She was still panting as she manoeuvred the bright orange office Chevette through the streets of the inner city. It was all the fault of the grape dress, really. If Julie hadn't started on that she might have left before the phone rang, and not learned that the plane was early, and not be chauffeuring a stomach-load of butterflies around now. It was always worse having to anticipate disaster.

She knew, however, that none of her clothes would have met with Julie's unqualified approval. The easy, comfortable blouse and skirt combinations were 'boring', the suits 'too severe', the dresses 'wallpaper clothes'. The root of the problem, according to Julie, was that Sarah lacked the prime motivation to dress fashionably: the desire to attract men.

As she swung out to pass a slow-moving container truck the tiny diamonds that studded her wedding ring caught the light and points of white fire blazed briefly, mocking her thoughts.

When she had first joined *Rags & Riches* as a nervous, inexperienced secretary Sarah had been grateful for Julie's help and advice. In fact she had spent her first few weeks' wages buying clothes, most of which, though dated, she still wore. Simon had made it clear that he resented the idea of her drawing money out of their joint account to buy clothes for a job he didn't want her to take, another petty attempt to make her feel guilty about wanting some independence. Yet when she had gone ahead and used her own earnings it had provided him with a fresh grievance . . . now she was trying to make *him* feel guilty and inadequate. Most of his complaints had been similarly confused and contradictory but at the time she had been too involved to see it and had suffered agonies of self-doubt as a result.

Her husband's death had come only four months after she had started her job and the resulting gradual ingrowth hadn't been a conscious process, but an instinctive reaction to inward and outward pressures.

A plane roared low overhead as Sarah turned into the airport approach road, reminding her of her mission, and she wished again that she knew something about the people she was to meet. Perhaps she could try some logical deductions.

She knew that Sir Richard Wilde was about 70, very rich and very famous. Therefore his son must be about 40, born with a silver spoon in his mouth, attending the best schools, gaining entrée to all the best places by virtue of his name. He would be sleek and well fed, impeccably dressed, of course, and probably rather aloof, as befitted his wealth and position. His companion would be much the same, perhaps the junior of the two.

There—they couldn't be too difficult to pick out of a crowd, thought Sarah smugly, especially as most of the flights from England at this time of the year were filled by families returning from Christmas reunions. And she had made her trip in record time—fifteen minutes.

Time is relative. To Max Wilde it seemed that he had been waiting an awfully long time and he found himself becoming increasingly irritated with each passing minute. Surely they would be met as arranged, in spite of the last minute change of plan? It was common courtesy, not to mention good public relations. He would allow the tardy Mrs Somerville another ten minutes.

Restlessly he shifted position in the cushioned chair. He felt flat, drained of energy. He shot an envious look at the man sitting next to him. Tom looked perfectly comfortable, quietly finishing off a cigarette, not at all depressed by the functional lifelessness of the terminal. The bulky body was relaxed, the heavy head tilted back, thinning grey hair fluffing out from behind large ears. He looked like a big, amiable teddy bear, but the simile was only apt in the physical sense. Tom's refined manners were anything but bearish and his brain, when it came to debits and credits and the ins and outs of tax laws, was the equivalent of a sophisticated computer. At the moment the computer was switched off, and Tom seemed to be very much looking forward to a few weeks of semi-relaxation in a Southern hemisphere summer. Max was not.

He only had himself to blame, of course. If he hadn't been so over-confident as to risk flying in marginal weather last April he wouldn't be facing exile now. It had been a needless risk and one that had very nearly ended in his death. And for what? For temporary gratification. For a woman whose body he enjoyed no more and no less than he had enjoyed others, and whose mind had begun to bore him utterly.

Max's social life had figured briefly in that last, blazing row he had had with his father before his rapid exit from London. Their relationship, always precarious, had suffered one of its recurrent blow-ups and this time Max, usually able to ignore his father's frequent provocative moods, hadn't even tried to avoid it.

He had arrived home from a particularly grinding session with the executives of a company that Wilde's was in the process of buying out. A number of problems had cropped up unexpectedly and it was nearing ten o'clock by the time he got into his car. Ice on the road had made driving a chore and negotiating his route Max regretted the impulse that had led him to agree to the meeting at the other company's offices. If it had been held at Wilde House he would have been only an elevator ride away from home.

By the time he reached the door of his penthouse apartment all he wanted was food, drink, sleep . . . not necessarily in that order. But he was greeted by Brandon, his butler, who apologetically informed him that his father was waiting in the study.

'Oh God, what has he come visiting for at this time of night?'

'He has been waiting some time, sir.'

'Lying in wait you mean. Bring me in a large brandy, will you? Nothing for Sir Richard, we don't want him to settle in.'

The study was his retreat, jealously guarded. Sir Richard had instructed that the apartment be designed as a showcase for Wilde Interiors and since Max spent so little time at home he made no demur. But he had put his foot down over the study and the quiet, understated elegance of the room contrasted with the dramatic brilliance of the living areas. Booklined walls and a long ebony desk warmed the deep-pile cream carpet and the cream velvet chesterfield. The wall behind his desk displayed a few favourites from Max's extensive art collection.

Sir Richard Wilde did not possess the kind of personality that complemented the room. Even seated at the desk, absorbed in some papers, he managed to radiate a volatile aura.

'You've been avoiding me for weeks, Max. I want to know why,' he announced, taking up the conversation as though they were already in the middle of an argument.

'Hello, father.' Max refrained from mentioning that he had been out of the country for most of that time. His father was well aware of the fact. Besides, it was true.

He walked over and twitched a paper out of his father's hand. 'Well, what is it that's so pressing it can't wait? Other than your enduring, endearing interest in my paperwork.' He flicked a sarcastic finger at the untidy pile on the desk.

His father squared off the papers with pale, neat hands while Max watched objectively. For the first time he noticed the thin black cane leaning against the edge of the desk and stifled a sigh. That meant his father was role-playing again. The aged parent, he supposed. It would be laughable if it were not so tiresome. Max was in no mood to play games.

'You're my son, my only child, of course I'm interested. I'm worried about you.' The quavery note was nicely balanced by an injured air.

'Well stop worrying,' Max said callously. 'I'm thirty-five not fifteen. I've been running my own life quite satisfactorily for a long time now. And if it wasn't for you I'd be running Wilde's the same way.' He turned and took the amber glass from a silent Brandon, approving the large measure with a dismissive nod.

He took a gulp, expecting a sour look from his father, but instead he got a quiet smile and the younger man's eyes narrowed. Usually a remark like that produced an explosion and usually Sir Richard, who only drank champagne, made some pointed remark about Max's drinking.

'That's exactly why I've come to see you. I can't put it off any longer, I wanted to tell you my decision right away.' He paused dramatically for effect. 'I'm getting on—sixty-eight at the end of next month—too old to be taking on a lot of unnecessary work.'

'Don't tell me you've decided to give up designing?'

He received a rigid stare. 'Don't be ridiculous. I'm an artist, artists never give up their work. Millions of women depend on me to dress them in a style to which they are unaccustomed.' His father's jokes were alway execrable. 'No, I'm talking about the business side of things. I've decided it's time you took over the chairmanship of the Group.' He sat back with the air of a magician who has just pulled a rabbit out of a hat, but the response was disappointing. Max refused to applaud.

'Indeed?' He walked over to the chesterfield and sat down, nursing his drink, contemplating his father. Tall and lean, like himself, Sir Richard was health personified. The desk lighting was flattering, but even in broad daylight his father didn't look his age. His face was lined, but they were the strong lines of character, and his hair, though white, was still the thick leonine mane it had been in his youth. His mind was as clear as a bell and he was still a powerhouse of energy.

He had talked about retiring before, but never seriously. In fact he had fought tooth and nail to retain his control, firmly resisting any efforts to dislodge him.

'And what are the strings?' inquired Max pleasantly.

'Strings?' Innocently. 'What strings? You're my son.'

'I've never known you offer anything without conditions. Perhaps you want me to merge with a textile heiress.'

'Don't be facetious, Max,' Sir Richard snapped, then stopped. 'Have you got someone in mind?'

'No, I have not.'

'Well, you should think about it anyway,' plunging down a sidetrack for a moment. 'A chairman should have a solid home background, the shareholders like it. Wenching is fine in your youth and I've no objection to the press you've been getting, but when you get to your age people begin to wonder if there's instability. You've got to start thinking about heirs, you know.'

'I don't have to do anything,' Max interrupted. 'I'm not marrying the first available candidate simply to provide you with grandchildren. In my considerable experience it's an overrated institution. Certainly you and mother were no blissful advertisement for the delights of matrimony.'

True to form his father waved the unpalatable away with an elegant gesture. 'Your mother was a very beautiful and intelligent woman but she could be very wilful.'

'As wilful as you.'

Sir Richard frowned. 'We're digressing. We're supposed to be talking about you. The fact is . . .' he reached for his cane and made a play of using it to haul himself up. Here it comes, thought Max, cynically. 'The fact is that my age is beginning to creep up on me. I can't be bothered with all these new angles your whizz kids are dreaming up . . . new companies, new directions. It's distracting and these days I need all my energy and concentration for my real work—designing. I had hopes, of course, that you would follow in my footsteps, but no matter, you've chosen other fields. Talent has many guises and I respect yours. You have a rational yet intuitive sense for business, you're demanding but fair, you have experience and all the qualities of leadership that would make you a good chairman.'

'Why do I get the feeling this is a funeral oration?'

'You have all these things,' his father continued inexorably, 'and yet, I hesitate. Why? Why do I now feel some doubt that you're ready for it?'

That brought Max up sharp. He set his half-empty glass down on the black coffee table beside him with a sharp click.

'What in the hell do you mean by that?'

'Just what I say. Something's not right, and I think you should tell me what it is. I should like to know, both as your father and as present chairman of Wilde's. For the past few months you've been like a cat on hot bricks, working like there's no tomorrow.'

'I've always worked hard. Dammit, you wouldn't want me as a director if I didn't pull my weight.' Max stood up abruptly, thrusting his hands into his pockets.

'I agree. But there is a difference between working hard and over-working. You're driving yourself close to the brink, physically and mentally.'

'Which one of your tame executives has been keeping tabs on me this time?' Max enquired caustically, aware that this was a rare reversal—he was losing control while his temperamental father remained cool. The thought only angered him more.

'It's not a matter of telling tales, Max, and if you were reacting less defensively you'd see that. If your health is in jeopardy, naturally that affects the companies you control and the people you employ. And this is not just a straightforward case of overwork. It's been going on ever since that crash. I can't put my finger on it exactly but you seem to have lost your sense of proportion. What you're doing doesn't seem to satisfy you any more and that worries me. What are you trying to prove, and to whom?'

'I'm not trying to prove anything!' Max was furious now. 'I don't have to. When I fail in my job, then you can worry. But don't accuse me of doing it too well.'

'But you're not doing it well, that's the point. Not as well as you used to. If you're not happy in your work how can you expect others to be happy working with you, or for you?'

'Thank you for the honesty—it's the company that's worrying you, not my personal welfare, so you can drop the aged parent act, it cuts no ice with me.'

Unabashed, his father abandoned the cane and stood tall. 'Up until now the two have been virtually indivisible, perhaps that's the problem. I built my empire out of blood, sweat and tears as well as talent, and I want you to inherit it. But more than that, I want you to want it as much as I did. I've never doubted your ambition or your determination to take over from me but if that changes, I want to be the first to know. I've seen too many good men crushed by the sheer weight of responsibility at the top to want to see it happen to any son of mine.'

'Is that what you think? That I'm cracking up? That I can't handle the responsibility any more?' Max demanded tautly. It was the nearest his father had ever come to conceding that Max was more than the extension of his own ambitions, but there was too wide a gulf between them now to bridge with words. Ever since he had left university Max had been aware that beneath the casual affection and respect they had for each other ran uneasy currents—a competitiveness that inhibited any real closeness between them and tempered trust with wariness.

'You tell me. Can you honestly say that there is nothing troubling you?' Sir Richard paused expectantly but Max merely compressed his lips. 'All right . . . I didn't expect that you would tell me. Perhaps you haven't even worked it out for yourself yet. Maybe you need time to think.'

'Not about the chairmanship.'

'Fine. Then there's something you can do for me before you take it on.'

'I knew there would be strings.'

'I've already discussed this with the other board members—individually, of course—and the consensus is that I resign at the March board meeting and you are voted in to my place. Naturally I'll still retain a seat on the board, but you will be Group Chairman. There'll be shufflings on some of the subsidiary boards as well, but when you come back we can discuss that further!'

'Come back!' Max rapped out. 'Come back from where?'

'New Zealand.' Sir Richard avoided his son's incredulous stare. 'You know that the publishing company has taken over this fashion magazine—*Rags & Riches*—there. I've been through the paperwork. It's a good little magazine, that's the general opinion, but it could do with a shot in the arm—hook it into our syndication network, inject a little more cash, that sort of thing. I see our first official issue is the April one; it will be going into preparation about now as a matter of fact, and will come out the week that we introduce the new collection in Australasia. Great possibilities there. I suggest you're the man to explore those possibilities. I want you to go down there, look at the situation, deal with it as you see fit. You've worked in this area before—you spent some time on *Elan* in Paris, as I recall, and enjoyed it, so you can't say it isn't in your line—'

'It isn't. Not now. Five years ago maybe!' Max exploded, unable to listen any longer. 'If you think you're going to exile me to the back of beyond until I shape up to some nebulous ideal—'

His father over-rode him with ringing tones. 'You can take your time. A month I think. You and Tom Forest.'

'So I get a nursemaid now! You're the one who needs the nursemaid, you must be going senile. I can't leave London now. I've got a thousand and one things on my plate. I'm not going to walk away from delicate negotiations now, it could kill a dozen deals.'

'We did without you while you were in hospital,' his father pointed out drily. 'You're not indispensable, Max, not yet anyway. As to your workload, that proves my point. I want the pressure off you for a while and I can't think of a better way of doing it, short of a complete holiday, and to get you to do that I'd have to commit you. You'll have one task and one task alone down there and I'll instruct head office to that effect. No long-distance conference calls. As for Tom, he damn well deserves time off. He's kept up with your pace in spite of the fact that he's more my generation than yours. I won't have you risking his health without good reason. If the thought offends your work ethic I suggest you get him to investigate the possibility of other interests Down Under.'

Max had the grace to feel uncomfortable. Tom had worked closely with him ever since Max had first joined Wilde's and had remained his right-hand man through all the learning years. Originally Sir Richard's man, he was now indisputably Max's; a source of sound advice and trusted wisdom, and taken too much for granted.

'If you don't want Tom, it'll have to be one of the whizz kids,' his father added cunningly and Max shook his head absently.

'Tom.' His head jerked up and he glared at Sir Richard when he realised the admission. His father was looking his usual sprightly self. 'What happened to creeping old age? Changed your mind about retiring?'

'My word is my bond.'

'And if I don't go I suppose you'll refuse to step down. I could force you to, regardless.'

'You could,' his father agreed complacently. 'But you won't. It would take time, you'd alienate a lot of good people and it would damage Wilde's reputation . . . not to mention me. But the choice is yours.'

'It's no choice, it's blackmail,' Max snapped and Sir Richard fell back on the age-old parental maxim:

'It's for your own good.'

Looking at it from a distance Max realised that if he had pursued his argument with his usual ruthless determination he would have prevailed in the end. In spite of his father's position and reputation Max wielded a great deal of power in his own right, not only in the votes of the many boards he was on but also in personal loyalty. He had never fully flexed his muscles because he had never needed to, and when it came to the point he had held back. And here he was, wondering whether he was going to regret it.

'You did inform Mrs Somerville it was Tuesday not Thursday, didn't you?' he asked Tom who had stood up to stretch his legs.

'The telex should have arrived first thing yesterday. I'll go and call their office, they may have got the times mixed.'

Max glanced at the flat silver watch on his wrist. 'It would be quicker just to find a taxi.'

'I'll phone first. Give them the benefit of the. doubt.' Ever the diplomat. Max watched as he disappeared in the direction of a row of telephone booths.

Easing the tension out of his neck and shoulders he began an idle survey of the comings and goings around him, noting the summer fashions. A woman coming through the automatic sliding door at the main entrance-way jolted him out of his torpor.

My God, if that's our typical New Zealand reader I can see our work cut out for us, he thought sardonically.

She hesitated and looked around. Max couldn't take his eyes off her, spellbound by a kind of detached horror. She looked about thirty years old but it was difficult to tell in that awful dress. The dated style did nothing for her and the muddy colour was further flattened by the deep tan of her skin. Her hair, scraped back into a severe pleat, emphasised the undistinguished features. Poverty, carelessness, or sheer lack of taste, decided Max critically.

He watched her walk briskly over to the British Airways

desk. Surprisingly, she moved well. His experienced eye detected that beneath that apology for a dress was a good body, tall and well-proportioned, though a trifle voluptuous for Max's taste.

He was still staring, lazily amusing himself by imagining what she would look like in some of his father's designs, when she turned impatiently from the desk attendant who was shaking his head. Their eyes met. Full face, the triangular line of her jaw and high cheekbones gave her a pointed, vulpine look and he smiled at the comparison.

He was rewarded with a cool disdainful look that held a hint of contempt. The kind of look that it was usually his prerogative to deliver. Caught on the raw he deliberately dropped his eyes in insolent appraisal of her body and when he raised them again he was gratified to see her reddening as she turned away. Her bag swung on her shoulder as she turned and he caught sight of the magazine tucked there.

Surely *she* couldn't be Julie Somerville? No fashion editor would be so unfashionable! However, it would be as well to check. He sighed.

Leaving his single case beside Tom's two bulging ones he picked up his briefcase and strolled over. He was half amused, half irritated to see her stiffen as she became aware of his presence and a slightly malicious impulse prompted him to make his first words ambiguous.

CHAPTER TWO

'ARE you waiting for someone?'

The voice was rich and brown, flavoured with harshness, like bitter chocolate. It made the back of Sarah's neck prickle oddly and, disliking the sensation, she turned defensively.

It was him of course. The man with the insulting stare. She had noticed him even before she entered the terminal, framed by the glass rectangle of the door. He was isolated from the rest of seething humanity as much by his expression as by the fact that he was sitting alone. No happy traveller there, but a world-weary cynic. The thin, dark face wore a look of intense boredom almost amounting to sullenness. His body was long and slim, disposing itself with an easy elegance, but the indolent attitude didn't entirely conceal the latent strength. He was dressed with a studied casualness—off-white linen shirt, open at the neck, and dark trousers. And he was attractive, sinfully so, in a dark, gypsyish kind of way.

He had watched her walk across the arrival lounge. She knew because she could feel it, just as she had felt his approach now. It had been a critical gaze too, and, irrationally, she had resented it. She was used to being superficially judged and found wanting by male eyes, usually it didn't bother her. But he did. And when she had seen that smile, that narcissistic expectation that she would smile back, overwhelmed with gratitude that he had condescended to notice her, she was seized by the desire to prick that peacock pride. And she had. His reaction to her non-reaction had been typical. Handsome men often thought themselves irresistible.

She lifted her chin and looked past him. 'Yes. If you'll

excuse me.' She made her voice as clear and cold as her slate-coloured eyes.

He moved at the same time she did, blocking her path, the smile tightening on his lips. At close quarters he was even more attractive. Sarah felt the impact of his masculinity as an almost physical threat and instinctively she shrank from it. A gypsy, but an aristocratic one, the slight signs of dissipation giving him an additional, dangerous, edge. The blue-black of his hair was reflected in the blue shadow on his chin and upper lip and there were shadows too under his eyes; those curious eyes that were not dark as one would expect, but light hazel, disturbingly brilliant.

'Do you mind? I said excuse me!'

'And I asked you a question.'

Sarah licked her lips. His persistence was vaguely menacing. 'I told you—'

'Excuse?' A pretty blonde British Airways stewardess materialised beside them and thrust a folded piece of paper at the man. 'Sorry I missed you when you left. Here's my number. If I'm not there my flatmate knows my schedule.' She flashed a brief, insincere smile at Sarah and dashed away again.

The man tucked away the piece of paper in his shirt pocket and raised a bland black eyebrow at Sarah.

'Now, where were we?'

'Nowhere!' snapped Sarah. She should have moved while she had the chance. Smug, egotistical devil! 'If you're so desperate for company why don't you catch another flight and collect a few more numbers!' The words sounded ridiculously priggish even to her own ears, but what with being late and not being able to spot her executives, and trying to cope with God's gift to women, she was rapidly losing what was left of her cool.

'I was going to suggest a good one for *you* to call,' he said evenly. 'A psychiatrist. You have quite an aggression problem there.'

'The one you go to no doubt,' responded Sarah sweetly. 'But doesn't he specialise? Egocentric males?'

There was a taut little pause.

'Are you always this rude to strangers?'

It was a farcical situation, exchanging insults in public with a perfect stranger. Already appalled by her uncharacteristic behaviour, Sarah searched for some way to defuse the conversation. Why hadn't she just ignored him, or frozen him off?

'Ah, there you are! You must be Sarah Carter. I've just been on the telephone to your editor.'

Sarah gratefully took the outstretched hand, smiling tentatively at her rescuer. Broad shoulders and a rather kindly middle-aged face.

'Mr Wilde?' she asked, questioningly.

His handshake was firm and dry and the polite smile widened appreciatively.

'I'm flattered, but no. I'm Tom Forest. Hasn't Max introduced himself yet.' He propelled her gently towards the other man. 'This is Max Wilde.'

In place of Sarah's brain sat a large chunk of marshmallow, pink and mushy and incapable of coherent thought. Luckily none of her body's other systems appeared to be working either—she didn't flush or stammer or burst into tears of humiliation. She just stood there and stared blankly at him.

'Pleased to meet you, Sarah Carter; at last.' The very lack of expression in the low, harsh voice was a mockery in itself. He extended a hand, like a challenge, and Sarah took it, avoiding his eyes by looking down at her hand almost engulfed by his. His knuckles whitened and she winced at the fierceness of his grip and looked up involuntarily to catch the gleam of amusement in his eyes.

He had known. All along he had known—or at least suspected—who she was. He had let her make a complete fool of herself and now he was enjoying her discomfiture. She fought in vain to stop the wave of heat from climbing into her face. She hadn't blushed in years and it was infuriating that this awful man should be able to make her do it twice within a few minutes.

'I'm sorry if you've been kept waiting.' Embarrassment rushed her into speech. 'But yesterday was the city's Anniversary Day, a public holiday. We didn't know about your change of plan until about half an hour ago.' An acceptable compression of time in the circumstances, she felt.

'It was rather short notice; and we haven't really been waiting long,' the older man replied, but with a quick glance at his companion that spoke volumes to Sarah. That expression of boredom hadn't been feigned.

'If . . . if you'll bring your bags and follow me—the car's right outside.'

She followed them over to their luggage. The two men were both the same height, but Tom Forest's large frame gave him an amble whereas Max Wilde glided with an almost feline grace.

The world outside was a vivid contrast to the controlled environment of the terminal. The warm humidity rolled into their faces with surprising suddenness and out in the direct sunlight colours everywhere seemed bright and hard.

'I think I'll go and find a cigarette machine,' Tom Forest said. 'I didn't buy any duty-free, I'm trying to give up. But I think I was a bit optimistic to think I could do it all at once. Now I've smoked my last one I think I need the security of an emergency pack.' With a smile he inclined his head at Sarah and she watched with regret as he walked away.

There was a long silence as Max Wilde moved forward and leant his forearms across the top of the car. He looked up into the arc of cloudless blue, narrowing his eyes against the glare. The heat from the metal soaked into his body soothing away some of the stiffness. The effects of the crash still lingered in his system even if, as his father had said, he didn't want to admit them. There were scars, not all of them physical, and considering the length the company went to play down the details of the accident, it was fortunate that there were no obvious disablements to explain away. Just this damned unsettling dissatisfaction with the world in general. Even the challenge of merger and takeover had lost its edge.

The longer the silence stretched, the more nervous Sarah became. What was he thinking about, to give his face that brooding, impatient look?

Damn the man! If she was going to be working with him for the next few weeks—working *for* him—she had better make her peace now and get it over with.

She cleared her throat. 'I'm sorry I spoke as I did just now, but I had no idea who you were . . .'

His head swivelled and for a moment she had the idea he didn't know who she was. Then the hazel eyes narrowed.

'Just a passing wolf on the prowl? Did you think I was moving in for the kill?'

'Of course not,' she floundered. She had, though goodness knew why. The man carried a positive masculine charge, he would never have to make the first move. Women, like that stewardess, would naturally gravitate towards his field of attraction. *Most* women, that is.

He inspected her again, with the curiosity of a scientist studying an interesting, but odd, specimen.

'You flatter yourself. Or is there something I don't see? Does every man who looks at you follow through with a pass?'

'That isn't what I—'

'Do you treat all men as potential rapists? It must make for a very exciting life.'

'Only the ones who look capable of it,' she rapped back, hating him for his deliberate taunts.

To her annoyance he merely laughed. 'From you that's a compliment, I'm sure. Sorry to disappoint you but public ravishment is not my style. I'm trying to remember what I read about you in the personnel files, nothing that prepared me for the unique quality of your welcome.'

If anything was calculated to haul Sarah up short, that was. What was she doing? Julie would *kill* her. And dance on her grave! How was she going to get out of this one?

'I'm—' The word jammed in her throat and took some pushing to release. 'I'm sorry . . . I—I'm not really back in the swing of things yet. I've only just come back from holiday. Everything was very much up in the air when I left. The deal must have gone through very rapidly.' She was beginning to babble but at least she wasn't saying anything that could be construed as insubordinate.

'I like to work quickly. It keeps everyone on their toes.'

'Are you going to be here long?' she asked, striving for normality.

'Long enough.'

'Have you ever been here before?'

'No.'

It was like trying to get blood out of a stone. Sarah made one last attempt. 'Well, you've picked the right time of year. February weather is usually the best of the summer.'

'I came here to work, not lie in the sun.'

'I'm sorry,' she said, dismayed by his sharpness. It seemed nothing she could do or say was right. She was always either insulting him or apologising to him. 'I was just making conversation.'

'Aimless chatter I can do without.'

Sarah would have liked to slap his supercilious face. Instead she gave him a brief vitriolic look which completely passed him by, and subsided into rigid silence.

Shortly afterwards Tom Forest arrived back, and together the two men loaded the three bags into the boot of the car. Max Wilde then got into the back seat with his briefcase while the other man eased himself in beside Sarah.

'You're Julie Somerville's assistant, aren't you?' he asked. 'Have you worked for *Rags & Riches* long?'

'Three years,' said Sarah, concentrating on her driving. An accident would really round off the morning! 'I started off as a secretary, the rest was sort of gradually accidental. Julie seemed to think I had the potential to do more than type letters and answer phones.'

'With the idea being that you eventually graduate to editor?'

'Oh no.' She had never ever thought about it. 'It's a job for a journalist and I'm no writer. I prefer what I do, which is a bit of everything and everything of little bits.'

'More managerial than creative.'

'Yes. But management involves creativity, too.'

The large head nodded thoughtfully. 'I'm glad you think so. Too often organisational skills are underrated. Not everyone has the flexibility to do it well, particularly when control involves the interaction of artistic temperaments.'

Sarah grinned. A very subtle way of saying the crazies who inhabit the extended world of fashion journalism.

They discussed the point in general terms for a while, then moved on to specifics—Sarah's job at *Rags* and the magazine itself. Aware she was being sounded out, she spoke honestly and intelligently, hoping the man in the back seat was listening. At least he wouldn't be able to dismiss her as brainless.

She could see him in the oblong of the rear-view mirror, head tipped back on the seat, eyes closed. The lines of tension around his mouth and eyes were quite pronounced and the rigidity of the jaw showed that even now he wasn't relaxed. She felt a moment's uncertainty. She should have made allowances for the fact that he had just spent nearly twenty-four hours in the air, been effusively humble instead of being offended at his sarcasm. Then she remembered that Tom Forest had been on the same trip and *he* had managed polite civilities at the end of it. Flashing another look at the closed face behind her, Sarah shivered. For all the charm that had lit his face when he had smiled at that stewardess, there had also been a certain cool calculation. Not a man given to impulse. Not a man to make an enemy of.

If only she hadn't been so hasty. She cringed to think of his incredulity when he realised she thought he was trying to pick her up. She would have to try and put it from her mind, try to forget, too, that instinctive dislike she had felt. It could make her job over the next few weeks very difficult and could even jeopardise her future with the magazine.

When they reached the hotel Sarah double-parked and offered to check in for them, but Tom Forest declined with thanks.

'We'll sort ourselves out and give Mrs Somerville a phone call,' he said. 'Thank you for meeting us, we'll see you again soon.'

Back at the office Sarah resigned herself to a wasted morning. Everyone wanted to know what the advance guard had discovered about the new arrivals. With difficulty Sarah managed a fairly accurate physical description and a less accurate description, because of the deliberate omissions, of her own feelings on meeting the great man himself. One by one her colleagues trotted back to their departments in the mistaken belief that they had pumped Sarah dry of information.

It wasn't until Julie got back from her meeting at ten-thirty that she really spilled the beans. Reluctant as she was to confess her stupidity, it was better that Julie heard it from her than from the Wilde man.

Wondering how to present her case Sarah had finally decided on a bald statement. Julie's sense of humour was a bit unpredictable and trying to dress up the facts as a funny story could well backfire.

Disbelief, annoyance, mock-sobs and heavy sarcasm was the result, followed by a short, sharp homily on the merits of being polite to strangers, even importunate ones. Quite mild for Julie, really.

'Honestly, Sarah, you are the limit,' she finished up. 'The one person I thought I could rely on not to foul up! What happened to your celebrated soft answer . . . the Carter trademark?'

How to explain about the prickle on the back of her neck? The instinct. The 'feeling'. She could imagine the beautiful blue eyes widen at such impracticality from practical Sarah. Besides, her complaint was quite justified, Sarah's job was to smooth down feathers that other people had ruffled, not do the ruffling herself.

'He should have introduced himself first,' she said, unwilling to take the entire blame. 'He definitely didn't look my idea of an English tycoon. More like a male model.'

'What did you expect—bowler hat and umbrella? Don't let the Hollywood looks fool you, honey. Men have done that before now and gone on to commit commercial suicide. He's got a brain with a capital B—commercial degrees up to here and the midas touch as far as money's concerned. Let's just hope he lists a sense of humour amongst his other attributes. I hope you apologised.'

'Of course I did!' She was not going to enlarge on *that* conversation.

Julie slammed drawers and shuffled papers noisily for a few more minutes and then to Sarah's relief she began to laugh.

'Here. You'd better take this.'

She tossed over a large green envelope. It landed with a soft 'phlop' on Sarah's desk, disgorging some of its contents—light cardboard sheets to which printed clippings were pasted. 'It's the file on Wilde's, you'd better do some homework.'

It took a while for Julie's mirth to subside. Sarah closed her eyes and ears to the distraction and settled down to read the file in front of her. It was certainly comprehensive. There were clippings from overseas newspapers and magazines, press-releases, notes and sketches from the various Wilde fashion collections as well as cross-references to letter and photographic files, which Sarah also looked through. She read through everything once, putting her speed reading to good use, sifting out the references to Max Wilde and putting them aside for further study.

From the tenor of the news reports she could deduce that his attitude to the press was ambivalent. When he wanted publicity for his ventures he appeared charmingly frank and forthcoming, welcoming questions. But equally, he could be a reporter's nightmare. 'Mr Wilde had no comment to make', 'Mr Wilde was unavailable for comment', 'Mr Wilde refused to answer further questions'.

Where his private life was concerned there wasn't even a 'no comment'. There were plenty of photographs—smiling, stern, frowning, quizzical—action flashes grabbed on the run, of him at nightclubs and theatres, fashion shows and functions. Always there was a beautiful woman on his elbow, or the suggestion of one just outside the frame, a slender hand clutching his, a wisp of skirt, the direction of his gaze. The captions were all gossip and heresay of the 'Millionaire Max's Latest Love' type. Sometimes there were coy little comments from the women in question but discretion was obviously something he expected from his female companions. Max himself never bothered to deny or confirm anything from what she could gather—not even the stories that were patently outrageous. Perhaps he knew that nothing generated publicity power like the suggestion of secrecy. His reticence made him a gossip columnist's dream.

Most of the financial news reports that mentioned him were also favourable, admiring even, in their restrained fashion and by the time Sarah had finished her homework she was sinkingly aware she had crossed swords with a very powerful and important man. However, nothing that she had read made her like him any better. All that money, all those boardroom and bedroom successes. How could he not be arrogant? Conceited?

It was some time before she became aware of the pangs of hunger and realised that it was lunchtime and she was alone in the office. She was just thinking of going out for a bite to eat when the phone rang.

'Sarah?' It was Julie, her voice raised over a background of restaurant clatter.

'Hello. I wondered where you'd got to.'

'A last minute luncheon engagement.'

Hearing the suppressed note of excitement in her voice, Sarah didn't have to ask with whom.

'Having met the man in the flesh I can sympathise with your crass idiocy of this morning. Fathomless charm. It would be interesting to plumb the depths.'

'Rather you than me.' Sarah hadn't even received a puddle of charm from the man. 'What time will you be back?'

'I don't know . . . I don't care,' floated the answer gaily. 'I probably won't be back at all. I cunningly brought an idea or two with me to run up the flagpole, so we may spend the rest of the afternoon saluting. Incidentally, he wants a full staff meeting tomorrow morning—send a memo out, will you? If anything urgent comes up, I'll be at the hotel. I'll see you this evening.'

'This evening?'

'You haven't forgotten the *Sappho* launching, have you? I sent the invitation out to you. I want you to be there, Sarah, it's a major new line.'

'More flag flying?'

'It's a good way of keeping up our contacts . . . learning what's going on in an informal way. Talking of which, I'm having an informal party on Sunday afternoon. Coming?'

Sarah hesitated. 'Of course.' Julie's Sunday afternoon barbecues by the poolside of her lovely home were legendary and few people passed up the chance to attend. Everything was very relaxed, you didn't even feel obliged to make conversation if you didn't want to. Just swim and eat and lie in the sun. The only type of party Sarah *did* enjoy.

'I had forgotten about tonight, thanks for reminding me. What time?'

'Seven. And Sarah?'

'Yes?'

'Wear something . . .' she sniffed, '*different*.'

Sarah hung up with a sigh. *Sappho* was a new cosmetics line coming on sale in New Zealand shortly and the American-based company was holding a 'happening' to introduce their product to the trade and media. They'd hired the top floor of the Intercontinental Hotel as the venue.

The trouble with me is that I'm becoming blasé about 'happenings', she told herself. As a novice she had gone to promotional evenings wide-eyed, but now they were just a small part of a full, demanding job.

CHAPTER THREE

By the time Sarah arrived at the Intercontinental Hotel everything was swinging. The noise-level was high, up-beat music competing with a voluble crowd, most of whom were watching a series of fantasy make-up demonstrations in one corner of the large restaurant. Drink was just as abundant as noise.

She greeted several people she knew and accepted a tall glass of something before being expertly cut out of the crowd by a young man from Sappho's advertising agency. Sarah glanced around the room while she listened politely, managing to look interested and impressed as she wondered whether the preponderance of unfamiliar faces meant the evening would be more of a chore than usual.

'Hello, Sarah. I wonder if I might have a word with you? Excuse us, Peter.'

Sarah was whisked away to the other side of the room by a pretty girl wearing a stunning combination of black lurex 'boob tube' and slinky, skin-tight gold satin pants.

'Thanks, I think he was just getting his second wind,' said Sarah gratefully. Her rescuer was one of *Rags*' staff writers.

'You looked as though you might be building up to a yawn. I would have come over sooner but I didn't want to break up what might have been a promising encounter.'

The two girls chatted for a few minutes about what Chris thought of the *Sappho* range, then a short speech signalled the end of the fixed agenda for the evening and the arrival of a mouthwatering array of food laid out on long, white-covered tables.

'Oh goody, I'm famished,' said Chris, who could eat

like a pig and never put on an ounce. She slanted Sarah a sly look. 'I don't suppose you have any room?'

'What?'

'A little bird tells me that you got your foot rather firmly wedged in your mouth this morning. Still there, is it?'

Sarah pulled a face. It had been too much to hope that Julie would keep her gaffe to herself, once she had seen the humorous possibilities.

'A little bird with a big mouth. I suppose it will be joke of the month now.'

'Are you kidding? Of the year! Did you really—!' She broke off to give Sarah a sharp nudge. 'Speak of the devil!'

Near the door at the other end of the room was Julie, still in yellow but looking as fresh as a daisy, her arm tucked smugly through that of the tall dark man.

'Oh, Sarah,' breathed the girl beside her. 'How could you?'

Very easily, thought Sarah, her nerves tightening a notch. The dark head was tilted to one side as Max Wilde listened to Julie's introductions. He looked totally at ease, the supreme confidence of power and wealth unmistakable. And the men he was meeting were shaking hands with the hint of deference that showed their awareness of it. He was wearing a dark suit, blue shirt and tie, yet he looked considerably cooler than many of the more casually dressed men around him. A state of mind rather than a physical condition, thought Sarah enviously.

'Lucky Julie,' drooled Chris. 'It looks like a take-over in more ways than one. Steven Somerville will have to look to his laurels. Hey!' Another nudge. 'He's looking at you! Give him a smile, Sarah.'

She had no choice. Forcing her reluctant cheek muscles into action she achieved a polite smile and inclined her head. To her intense embarrassment, conscious of the audible gasp beside her, he made no answering sign of recognition. He continued to look straight through her for several moments, a blank expression on his face. Then he turned away.

Sarah's whole body burned as she stared unseeingly at the back of his head, feeling as if the whole room had witnessed that snub. She knew precisely what he was doing—paying her back in kind, but most unkindly, and unfairly. In the midst of her angry embarrassment she was surprised that he would stoop to such a thing. Perhaps spite was part of his nature—look how he had enjoyed watching her squirm at the airport when she found out who he was.

'Do you think he didn't recognise you?' Chris looked from Max Wilde to Sarah's pale face. 'It's a big room, maybe he's short-sighted.'

In a pig's eye! thought Sarah, but she didn't say it. Stout-hearted Chris was unwilling to think badly of anyone, particularly a man whom, she had cheerfully informed everyone that morning, she had lusted after for years from afar.

'He was probably miles away,' Sarah said stiffly.

'Sure. But—'

'Forget it, Chris.'

Sarah could see her friend was dying to ask a flood of questions, but those three final words told her she would get nowhere. Her colleagues knew that there were clearly defined lines within which it was unwise to step where Sarah was concerned. One heavily scored line involved men and her personal relationships with them, her husband included. Sarah could take good-natured ribbing with the best of them but real curiosity was an intrusion. Because they liked and respected her they obeyed the unwritten rule, knowing that Sarah reciprocated by respecting the privacy of others.

'Okay, but seeing as you're obviously not going to introduce me, I'll drift on over myself. Maybe I can pry him away from Julie long enough to try my luck!'

Luck would have nothing to do with it, Sarah decided as she elbowed her way through to the buffet. That man made his own luck! His arrival seemed to have taken her appetite away but she piled her plate with chilled oysters in the shell, crayfish mayonnaise and salad, anyway. She would eat every scrap, just to prove to herself that it made no difference what he thought or did to her. She wasn't going to let herself be intimidated by someone else's opinion. It had happened once before in different circumstances and had brought nothing but stress and strife.

She had almost finished her meal and was sitting alone at her table after sharing it with a succession of companions, sipping on a light, cold white wine, when she suffered the shock of seeing Max Wilde sit down on the vacant chair opposite.

At her sharp intake of breath some of the wine went down the wrong way and sent her into a fit of coughing and spluttering, eyes watering furiously. The man was a jinx!

'Drink some more wine.'

She did as she was told and immediately felt better. Why did her common sense desert her in his presence?

'All right?'

She nodded, not trusting her voice, hating that grin.

'Good.' He sat back. 'Lost your tongue? Or minding your manners? How did it feel to be on the reverse end of a glacial stare?'

Struggling for composure, Sarah stole Chris's line without compunction. 'You mean when you arrived?' She shrugged casually. 'I assumed you must suffer from short-sightedness.'

He followed her further than she meant him to: 'And too vain to wear glasses?' She got a view of a hard, olive throat as he drew back his head to laugh uninhibitedly. If Sarah hadn't disliked him so much she might have found it an attractive sound. 'Nicely said. Unfortunately—for you—I know you better than to believe you thought anything so innocent.'

'What makes you think you know me at all?'

Lids veiled the glitter of his eyes. 'I told you. I've read your file.'

He made it sound like a scandal sheet, although Sarah knew it only contained unadorned facts and figures.

'And I've read yours, Mr Wilde,' she said, imitating his tone.

'Checking up on me?'

'It's part of my job to know what's going on.' Perhaps the conversation could be steered on to more conventional lines. She must remember what Julie said about him, albeit in rather exaggerated terms: 'He's life or death for us, sweetie. We don't need the extra aggro that antagonising him could give us. Be *nice* next time you see him.' Sarah would as lief be as nice to a tiger. This one had intelligence as well as speed and strength; a wicked combination.

'Then you didn't do your job very well this morning, did you?' he replied, not diverted.

'There were circumstances . . .'

'Julie explained,' he cut her off. 'What conclusions did you come to then, about me, from your file?'

'None,' she lied. 'I prefer to make my own judgements.'

'So do I. That's what I'm doing now.' Just the kind of remark to set her at her ease! 'Do you like your job?'

'Yes.' He must know that already if he had listened to her conversation with Tom Forest.

'Ambitious?'

'In what way?' she asked carefully.

'How many ways are there?'

Sarah licked her lips. Why couldn't she treat him as she did any other person showing a casual interest in her job?

'I suppose I'm ambitious in that I want to be the best at what I do.'

'That's not ambition, that's human nature. Ambition is *needing* to be the best. According to Julie you're the best Editorial Assistant she's ever had, and that includes her stints in New York and Paris.'

His voice was slightly dry and Sarah searched his face for signs of sarcasm. There were none. Mind you, he was only repeating what Julie said, not complimenting her.

'She demands a lot and usually gets it,' Sarah said, giving credit where it was due. 'Julie's taught me practically everything I know.'

'I doubt whether modesty was included.' That touched a chord of humour in Sarah but she didn't let herself smile. 'What about writing? If not being a journalist precludes you from editorship—' he *had* been listening '—do you not feel your job self-limiting?'

'No. There are other directions. I didn't want to be a writer, I still don't.'

'No talent?'

'No inclination.' Annoyed. Writing was like offering up a part of yourself on a platter for the world to pick over. Sarah had never even been tempted.

'Then you don't have any frustrated ambitions?'

'Why should I? Ambition isn't everything.'

'It is if there's nothing else,' he murmured and Sarah met his enigmatic gaze. Once again she had the feeling that for him, for the moment, she didn't exist. Had she imagined that faint bleakness?

'Well, I suppose wanting to be happy is an ambition, and in that sense everyone is ambitious,' she said slowly, looking out of the window at her elbow. The view was quite spectacular, the city below settling into dusk, lights beginning to prick on in the streets which criss-crossed down to Quay Street and the bright port illuminations. Over on the North Shore, beyond the out-flung arm of the harbour bridge, comfortable suburbia was also lighting up and to her right Sarah could see the shadowy hulk of Rangitoto Island receding into the darkening sky.

Unconsciously, Sarah's voice had contained the gentle reassurance that she had so often used when Simon was suffering from bouts of inadequacy, real and imagined. It was an automatic response that would have worried and disturbed her if she had realised she was doing it. She didn't, but the man opposite did, and was struck by the irony of this odd, prickly female offering him reassurance. His curiosity was aroused, too.

'That most difficult of all ambitions to achieve,' he said, prompting softly.

Yes. And the most fleetingly held. It ran like dry sand between your fingers . . . one moment you had it warm and soft in your hand, the next it was gone. Sarah's happiness with Simon had been like that. And now she had found a new, different kind of happiness. Contentment. But already she could hear the rustling flurries of a rising wind that threatened to disturb it. Nothing stayed the same, no matter how much you wanted it to.

'Don't you think so?'

'I—' With a shock Sarah realised that she had nearly said what she was thinking, spoken the unspoken fear out loud. The shutters dropped immediately and the eyes which had been almost sea-green became hard as pebbles.

'Perhaps.'

'Perhaps?' His mouth twisted. 'You don't want to agree with me but you don't like to disagree. I think I preferred it when you were spitting at me, at least you were being honest.'

'There are times when honesty defers to diplomacy,' said Sarah undiplomatically, still agitated by the way he got under her skin.

'Fortunately I'm not hampered by any such restriction. Tell me, do you deliberately dress like that or is it merely innate bad taste?'

Sarah's jaw nearly dropped at his incredible affrontery. New Zealanders were generally a tolerant race with a 'live and let live' philosophy that usually enabled them to accept people as they were. It wasn't often that people remarked on Sarah's personal appearance, other than those who knew her well enough to essay a gentle joke or, like Julie, adopt a maternal exasperation.

'I'm sorry if the way I dress doesn't meet with your high standards, Mr Wilde,' she said stiffly. 'But it really isn't any of your business.'

'I think it is. You work for me, remember? Or you will in

a couple of months; and you're a rather poor advertisement for a fashion magazine.'

'I'm not advertising anything. We employ other people to do that. It isn't a condition of my employment that I make the Best Dressed lists. My clothes are perfectly respectable.'

'Oh, they are,' he agreed pleasantly. ' "Respectable" is the kiss of death as far as fashion is concerned. You don't deny, I notice, only defend.'

'I dress as I please,' said Sarah desperately. She could feel her grip on the conversation slipping.

'Then you're too easy to please. I'm not. But this is neither the time nor the place to discuss it. I can see your editor looking anxiously over this way. Smile, or she'll think you're saying something she'll regret later.'

Sarah resisted the urge to look furtively over her shoulder. He had a nasty habit of springing verbal surprises, the kind that left you hanging over a cliff wondering where the solid ground had gone.

'Julie knows me better than that.'

'And knowing you, wouldn't expect you to smile, mmm?'

Sarah stared at him for a moment, then out of sheer perversity switched on a brilliant smile, the kind that she had seen Julie use on less-than-intelligent men. Except Julie also fluttered her eyelashes slightly and Sarah couldn't quite bring herself to do that. Besides, her soft, natural ones wouldn't be quite as impressive as Julie's artificial abundance.

'Why, Mr Wilde, whatever gave you that idea?' she said coyly. If he wanted her to pander to his ego, she would comply, with a vengeance!

Being more than intelligent he immediately got the point. But his reaction wasn't what Sarah expected. She had half hoped, half feared he would be annoyed, but he wasn't. He showed a very genuine amusement, appreciative of the way she had very neatly turned the tables.

'Touché,' he acknowledged. 'I fear my pique was show-

ing. I won't ask you to smile again. I'll leave it to your
discretion. You're right of course, a response must be
spontaneous to be honest. I believe that a person's instinctive reaction to a given situation is a far truer indication of
their nature than a modified response, which is a social
imposition.'

Like this morning, for instance, Sarah thought. Is that
what he was saying? And just now – that urge to annoy
him by simpering like a feather-brained idiot? If so, Sarah
didn't agree; social conventions were important, they
protected, restrained, aided inter-personal relationships.
Following your instincts was dangerous and often wrong.
Wasn't her attraction to Simon instinctive? And also her
initial reaction to his possessiveness—to be flattered, to
baby him out of it instead of standing up for herself?

Deep, dark thoughts and she resented Max Wilde for
making her think them. A tactical withdrawal was called
for. She should have kept her mouth shut from the first.
Been *nice*. *Modified* her responses. He would have been
none the wiser.

Sarah looked at the dark countenance now in profile.
He certainly was a handsome man. No, she corrected
herself, not handsome—beautiful, yet in no way feminine.
There was a fine-boned, thoughtful arch to the brow and
the hard, high cheekbones and hawkish sweep of the nose
gave him a touch of nobility. Those strange eyes were
fringed with thick, dark lashes and the tanned skin was
smooth and finely grained.

His hair was straight, trimmed just above his collar,
jet-black but for the gleam of grey in the short sideboards.
The etchings of strain around the features were deepened
by tiredness; the cynicism she guessed was habitual. A
man of culture, a man of passion . . . The mouth and eyes
held sensual promise, a promise that from all accounts
had been often made and probably just as often fulfilled.

Seated, he still retained a grace of carriage and poise
that reminded her of a dancer; an alert, controlled, poten-
tially explosive strength masked by grace.

At precisely that point in her thoughts he turned his head, quite casually, and she was caught openly staring. Sarah's throat closed in the grip of an unidentifiable fear and every muscle in her body tensed. The room receded and his image came into ultra-sharp focus, claustrophobically close, and her heart thumped hot and heavy as the moment stretched into eternity.

Simultaneously, they both looked away and Sarah discovered that she had been holding her breath . . . waiting. For what? She released her breath slowly, carefully, wondering what he had seen in her face. Had that panicky feeling showed? She glanced surreptitiously at him out of the corner of her eye but the classic profile was unreadable. She was being overly-sensitive, allowing a vague apprehension to run away with her. Everything would be all right tomorrow. She would be back in a familiar environment, on her home ground, when she met him next. And he would have other things to concern him, to draw his attention; Sarah could sink gratefully into the background again. Let Julie answer his questions, deal with his unpredictability!

Sarah got up, clutching the wooden back of the chair. 'If you'll excuse me, Mr Wilde, there are several people I should speak to . . .' He looked up again, eyes light and faintly mocking.

'Of course. I'm sure there'll be plenty of other opportunities for conversation.'

It sounded like a threat, and as he rose Sarah slipped away. She didn't know whether he was watching her, but the back of her neck was prickling like mad as she skirted the couples now disco-ing on the dance-floor. Once she was screened from him by the crowd she broke for the door.

'Leaving already, it's only nine?' It was Julie, eyeing Sarah's batik skirt with disfavour.

'I think I've done my share of flag flying.'

'Okay; at least you came. Did you tell everyone about tomorrow's meeting?'

Sarah nodded.

'Good. Good. Er . . . What did he say?'

Max Wilde must have been telling the truth about the anxious look. Sarah hesitated. 'That you'd explained about this morning. I think we cleared the air.' She crossed her fingers.

'Terrific!' Julie beamed. 'He was very reasonable about it, you know, considering it wasn't his fault. We had a little laugh over it and everything was as smooth as apple pie.'

Had a little laugh about it! Sarah repeated savagely to herself as she rode down in the lift, changing a frown to a polite smile as a clutch of Japanese businessmen boarded at the next floor. Smooth as apple pie! What did Julie know? He hadn't withered her with sarcasm, or snubbed her, or laughed at her! Julie *liked* him.

Sarah didn't. Not at all.

CHAPTER FOUR

As the week came to a close Sarah told herself that at least she had tried. Julie couldn't fault her for that. She had attempted to be as pleasant, co-operative and efficient as usual, but the good ship *Resolution* foundered in the sea of unpredictability that was Max Wilde. Self-effacement didn't work with him, he liked to make waves, get opinions—provoke them, if necessary. He certainly seemed to take delight in provoking Sarah out of her cool composure.

The constricting self-consciousness she felt in his presence got worse. She dropped things, and forgot things, and made stupid mistakes, all of which made her even more nervous. It was a vicious circle.

Grudgingly she had to admit that as an Executive Editor he knew his stuff. He immersed himself in the job as though it was the most challenging of his career, and in doing so challenged the *Rags* team to keep up with him. He worked with aggressive speed, absorbing information like a sponge, tapping the minds around him and handling the reins of command with easy confidence. He made himself approachable, yet had sufficient presence to instil respect. And he was a master at the art of persuasive reasoning, the subtle manipulation of argument in his own favour.

By Friday the tacit agreement was that however dynamic a brain he was, Max Wilde wasn't an easy man to work for. He was uncomfortably impatient – smiling one minute and snapping the next. Wherever he went he created a natural surface tension which Sarah found as irritating as it was stimulating.

After the first burst of hyper-activity he settled down to mere over-activity. Surely he didn't work at this sort of intensity all the time? Not even the devil himself could keep that up, thought Sarah, appalled by his sheer drive. No wonder he had been curious about her ambitions, and so sceptical when she said she hadn't any. Work to him was as natural as breathing and he regarded everything in the light of a debit or credit.

He was generous with praise where it was due, quick to appreciate a good idea. But he was also extremely caustic in his criticisms, and brusque to the point of rudeness with excuses, however justified. He did not suffer fools gladly and at times used words like weapons, striking straight to the heart of the matter regardless of personal feeling, exposing hidden weaknesses and dealing with them ruthlessly. It was unpleasantly like a trial by ordeal to be on the receiving end of his critical dissection, as Sarah found out on several occasions.

It didn't help that he continued to make derogatory remarks about Sarah's clothes or that he seemed to be amused by the references to the manner of their meeting. He may have forgiven, but he wasn't forgetting!

On Friday morning Sarah arrived at work to find that Julie and Chris, together with two more colleagues, Nora and Mike, were already settled around the big oval oak table in the interview-cum-conference room. Sarah was about to take the seat nearest the door when Marie and Keith arrived and Sarah took a playful swing at the art director with her note pad. He executed a neat side-step and to her horror she ended up hitting Max Wilde himself, who was following close behind. It was only a light tap but it hit him squarely in the chest.

'Sorry,' she blushed, and hurriedly sat down, trying to avoid seeing Keith's smirk.

Max Wilde, in a grey suit and shirt but without a tie, looked slowly around the table before uncapping the nib of a silver pen. Like unsheathing a sword, Sarah thought.

'Let's get straight down to business, shall we? I'm impressed, both by your obvious commitment and by some of the ideas you have put forward for this.' He indicated the artist's board beside him displaying the *Rags* mock-up. 'However, I have some points to make. The emphasis I question. You're changing masthead, layout, typeface—all the things that are your signature. All right, change the cover to indicate your new affiliation, change the order of your columns and add new ones, but not the type. It's clear, it's clean, it's *Rags*. Changing it would be too much of a shock for your readers. Certainly we want to startle, to challenge, but not to shock.

'The content is a different story. You have tried to broaden the base of your appeal, but you haven't gone far enough. You've put in furniture, interior decoration— why not food and wine? They're also part of *ambience*.'

'But we're a fashion magazine, a specialist magazine,' Nora interjected.

'How specialist is fashion? It's custom; not only of dress, but of manners, of tastes in everything—even thought. Think of your name. You're not only *Rags* you're *Riches* too. Money and everything that it can buy. In fact, why not have a regular financial column, money from a woman's point of view—how to get it, invest it, enjoy it?'

That interested Chris, who was knowledgeable about stocks and shares and bought jewellery as an investment. She was always telling Sarah that it was important to make your money work for you. But her advice fell on stony ground. To Sarah money was something you either banked or spent.

Having tossed his suggestions into the ring, Max Wilde now sat back and watched the dogfights that ensued. The pale eyes followed the rapid exchanges with a piercing intensity and the slim fingers played ceaselessly with the pen. Sarah found her eyes drawn to that little bar of silver as it was twisted and twirled, rolled back and forth and occasionally used to make notes. She had rarely seen him completely still, except just before he pounced on an unfortunate victim of his displeasure, like a predator pausing to judge speed and distance.

Although she wasn't taking any part in the discussion herself, Sarah listened closely. She had heard these arguments many times before but seldom with the sense of urgency they had now. This time what they said would have meaning and effect, it wasn't just letting off steam, stirring the creative juices with complaint and argument.

Sarah began doodling on her pad with her very prosaic ballpoint, sketching the man at the end of the table with reasonable proficiency. Simon had been quite helpful when she had mentioned she would like to learn to draw, but his fiercely professional criticisms of her dabblings had defeated their own purpose. The enclosed room was very warm and Sarah blinked hard as she added horns and a tail to complete the picture. For some reason she hadn't been sleeping very well lately.

'Are we boring you, Sarah?'

Her pen slid off the paper and she straightened in her chair.

'Of course not.' The give-away was her voice, squeezed high by the yawning bubble that had frozen in her throat. 'Just making notes.' She tilted her pad sharply away from Keith who was craning for a look.

'Good,' came the crisp reply. 'Then you can make a few comments.'

'I . . . really haven't been involved in the new developments. I was away—'

'I know. But you must have formed an opinion. You have some very definite opinions, and you have been making copious notes. Enlighten us, please.'

The voice was redolent with sarcasm and Sarah felt even more like a recalcitrant schoolgirl caught cribbing at an exam. Some of the faces around the table grinned expectantly as the prospect of some entertainment loomed.

'I haven't had time to study the mock-up in any detail—'

'Even better. Your regular readers won't get time to study it either, before they're presented with the *fait accompli*. What are your first impressions?'

'Well . . .' she pretended to look down at her nonexistent notes to give herself time to curb her wayward mind. 'I did think the changes a bit dramatic, especially, as you said, the typeface . . .'

'I think I can guess that you would prefer to retain the status quo. But putting the preference aside for a moment, what about some constructive comment,' came the dry response.

'That is constructive,' Sarah protested. 'Our circulation figures are holding steady, surely that's a vote in favour of the status quo.'

'Holding steady is another way of saying remaining static. You're keeping your hard-core readers but not acquiring new ones.'

'But we can only expect to hold a certain percentage of the market.'

'A percentage you haven't quite reached yet. And there's the floating buyer, the one you have to grab at the magazine stand with an eye-catching cover and the promise of good, readable, varied material within. *Rags* has been on the market long enough to be secure, familiar. Now is the time to stimulate the reader by adding a little unfamiliar spice.'

'Why not herbs instead of spice? They have a more subtle flavour.' One part of Sarah's mind noted that he had stopped fiddling with his pen. Was that a good sign or bad?

'Specify.' That singular challenge he was so fond of issuing: explain yourself, talk, convince me. Now she was started she would not retreat. She might be wary about caring for people, but she cared *about* them, about *Rags* and its readers and contributors.

'I don't like Male of the Month,' she said baldly to a chorus of disapproval.

'It's a great idea,' cried Chris. 'It'll be tremendous fun to do.'

'Don't be such a stick-in-the-mud, Sarah,' said Julie. 'Everybody's loosened up these days. It's really just male fashion shots with a bit of personality thrown in.'

Backed into a corner Sarah came out fighting.

'It's not the idea that I don't like,' she told the room at large. 'It's the way it's presented. It's the worst kind of sexism.'

'I might have known you were an ardent women's libber,' came from the head of the table.

'If that means I have confidence in our women reader's intelligence and taste, yes I am,' Sarah shot back.

'What is it precisely that a woman of intelligence and taste would object to?'

The dry cynicism infuriated Sarah. He had asked for her opinion, hadn't he?

'The whole tenor of the article. The captions are pure cheesecake. It may be fun to write, but I think it should be more than just a stereotyped joke.'

'You mean . . . take it seriously?' asked Julie sceptically.

'More or less. A sophisticated version. A mood interview piece. There are plenty of attractive men around—' she ignored the laughs and whistles, '—from entertainers, to politicians, to businessmen, to the stranger in the next car at the red light. Each month let's get a guest columnist to take out the man of her choice and do an impressionistic story about the evening. Team it with one big colour shot and a few black and white and you have . . .' she searched for the words as her enthusiasm for the idea outran itself.

'The ultimate female fantasy,' Julie finished for her. 'Sometimes, Sarah, you really surprise me. I like it! I like it very much. It could be very sexy.'

'Bags I go first,' laughed Chris. 'The perfect excuse to ask a man for a date, and on expenses too!'

A light-hearted squabble broke out, relieving the strain of the past hour or more of vehement discussion. Even Max Wilde relaxed, as much as he was able, chin resting on his steepled fingers, looking every inch a candidate for Male of the Month. Maybe she should suggest it, thought Sarah with an inward giggle, knowing he would detest the very idea. But what a scoop it would be! She was very, very tempted, thinking of all the times he had been provocative, but bit hard on her tongue. Giving in to impulses like that to annoy him invariably got her in over her head, he merely took it as a sign that he was succeeding in getting under her skin. Which he was dammit! She already spent too much idle time thinking up crushing remarks with which to slam the stable door after the mocking devil had bolted.

Back at her desk after the meeting had broken up, Sarah quickly searched out some documents, intending to slip along to Tom Forest's room at the end of the corridor and inveigle him out to a conveniently early lunch. She was not fast enough, however, because when she looked up Max was standing in front of her desk. He was only half a head taller than she was but he always seemed to *loom*. Come to that he loomed even when he was sitting at his desk which had been placed for his use several paces away. It was most unnerving. Sarah was used to meeting men on her own level, often looking down on them. It was easy to be firmly off-putting to a man who was shorter than you. This one was not only tall, but tenacious, with a visible aura of masculinity that offended Sarah as much as his on-again off-again charm did.

Simon had had charm; getting his own way was easy. Until Sarah discovered that he used it the way he used everything—temper, depression, jealousy—as therapy. He worked out his moods by manoeuvring people into responding in a certain way and then attacking them for it. It gave him a sense of power when his own self-respect was at its lowest ebb. Only when Sarah had refused to play the game, had been angry at his charm, laughed at his depression, shrugged at his jealousy had the real person begun to emerge. But by then it was too late, Sarah's emotions had been exhausted into apathy. Charm was merely one of the trappings of personality, no guarantee of inner warmth or depth.

To Sarah's dismay Max Wilde leaned over until his face was only inches from hers. He spoke with a slow precision that was more alarming than his fiery spurts of temper.

'Just once I would like to see you react to me naturally, and smile as though you mean it, not just out of politeness, or as a weapon. I don't like it when you're polite and silent. It makes me curious to know what is going through that oddly constructed brain of yours.'

Sarah shied backwards, almost knocking over her chair in the process. His words were obscurely threatening but at least it was some consolation to know that he wasn't omnipotent. Her thoughts were still safely wrapped up inside her head.

He sauntered over to his own desk and sank into the scoop-backed chair, legs outstretched, crossed at the ankle, acting as a pivot for the slight movement of the swivel. With his hands still in his pockets he looked a picture of indolence. Sarah, tense and wary, recognised the all-too-familiar signs. Eyes half closed, jaw muscles relaxed, mouth deceptively bland—he was about to indulge in some Sarah-baiting. Killing time until lunch.

'What I can't quite reconcile,' he said lazily, 'are those two images, the outraged spinster of Tuesday and the rational, liberated Mrs Carter of this morning who has sufficient worldly wisdom to recognise the subtle power of the intellect. The appeal of the sensuous over the merely sensual . . . that was the gist of your argument about the Male of the Month, wasn't it?'

She hadn't thought of it in precisely those terms, but in essence that was exactly it. However, she had no intention of being drawn into agreement or anything else with him. He could tie her up in verbal knots, and who knew what she would end up admitting.

'I really must go . . .' she said, gathering up the papers she had been looking for, and her handbag, but he wasn't listening. He suddenly seemed to find the gleaming black tip of his shoe interesting.

'Two images,' he said softly, and his eyes narrowed even further, then closed altogether. In spite of his olive skin, the lids had an almost translucent quality and Sarah felt a strange disquiet on seeing the delicate blue tracery just under the bony ridge of the eye socket. She didn't want to think of him as flesh and bone and blood, a man. He was an adversary, someone—a person—she neither knew nor liked. She didn't ask herself why.

She was almost out the door when he spoke again, his voice no longer soft.

'One more thing, Sarah.'

'Yes?' She half turned to show she wasn't coming back into the room.

'My name is Max. Use it. You're the only one who doesn't. You don't call me anything, but you know very well who I am.'

'Very well—' but it still wouldn't come. She wasn't even aware of giving him a name in her thoughts. Ridiculous when she called Tom, older and more deserving of the respectful 'Mr', by his first name.

He smiled unkindly. 'It'll come. Practise at home, in front of the mirror.' He looked at the dark green skirt and blouse she wore. 'If you have one, that is.'

Even a leisurely lunch with Tom, talking about the points of interest he should see during his visit, couldn't completely banish the sting of that last remark.

CHAPTER FIVE

THE first few moments of consciousness, before she opened her eyes, were the most precious; her mind still adrift among the soft rags of dreams, her senses beginning to register the beckoning warmth of a new day. Summer Sunday mornings were sweet and ripe and made to be enjoyed with slow pleasure.

Tossing back the feather duvet Sarah pulled on a cotton robe. She would breakfast outside.

A few minutes later she carefully mounted the black wrought-iron staircase that spiralled from the dining area to the upper floor, a bowl of muesli and fruit in one hand, a cup of steaming black coffee in the other.

She slid open the ranchslider and settled down on the sun-warmed canvas chair on the balcony, resting her coffee cup on the low wooden divide which separated the stretch of decking next door from her own.

As she ate she surveyed her domain. The sun was well clear of the horizon but it was still quite early, the air fresh and unsullied by the racketings of the human race, except for the quiet purposefulness of the morning church-goers and the far-off meanderings of yachties out pursuing their salty pleasures in the aquamarine bowl of the harbour. A few clouds punctuated the sky but they were innocent flosses of cotton candy, weightless, seemingly unmoving, though the white sails below were plump with satisfying breezes.

'Waiting for me, my love?'

The muesli tilted dangerously as Sarah jumped, hearing echoes of another time, another place.

'Quite the contrary, Roy. Go away and leave me in peace.'

Roy Merrill's face, what could be seen of it under thick curling red hair and full matching beard, creased in a grin. He rested stocky, ginger-frosted forearms on the divide and took a sip from her cup, pulling a face at the bitterness.

If one trusted apparel to proclaim the man then Roy, bare-chested and in faded, paint-encrusted cut-off jeans, was easy-going, good-natured and somewhat disreputable. But he was also intelligent and talented; meticulous even—but only on canvas. To Sarah he was the brother she had never had, the one person who seemed to understand her feelings. He was certainly the only man she felt comfortable with, for he had never shown the slightest sign of being interested in her as a woman. That, she supposed, was the strength of their relationship, their complete physical indifference to each other, and their mutual respect. That was how they could live in such close proximity, wandering into each other's home at will, with an easy intimacy uncomplicated by tension.

Considering that he had been such a friend of Simon's, the accord between them was surprising, but it had always been so. Roy, American-born and educated, had been a guest tutor during Simon's first year at art school and had been one of the few people to get really close to the young man, nurturing his talent and using his own well-known name to further his protégé's career. They had even moved into the adjoining town houses when Simon had inherited several thousand dollars and been able to match Roy's investment, an arrangement which had suited them professionally as well as privately.

From the first, Sarah had felt that Roy accepted her as a person in her own right, not just as his friend's wife, and after Simon died their affection for each other had not changed. Roy had been unstintingly kind and asked nothing in return, not even questions. She knew that he was concerned about her, especially since he had been the one to break the news about Simon that awful night, the one to whom she had sobbed out her fear and anger and grief. But he had conspicuously respected her silence since. Until a few months ago. Until now.

'I can't go away, honey,' he said. 'We had an appointment. Remember?'

She did. Too well.

'I haven't finished my coffee.'

'I'll do that. I haven't had any breakfast.' Roy was incredibly cavalier about his eating habits. He wasn't above making midnight raids on Sarah's refrigerator, which was well-stocked for just such an eventuality, when working late and smitten by a hunger that wouldn't be satisfied with beer and cold baked beans. 'I'll just go and empty a packet of sugar into this while you climb over.'

'I'm still in my nightie,' she called desperately as he disappeared inside his own sliding door.

'You're wearing more than me then,' came the answering call and Sarah sighed. He had finished the painting two weeks ago. She had to see it some time.

She finished her muesli first . . . she might need the blood sugar. She was just as reluctant now as she had been five months ago when Roy first asked her to pose for him. Not out of embarrassment, for having moved in artistic circles for three years she had acquired a very practical approach to life studies and she had posed many times for Simon. It was a measure of the almost schizophrenic nature of her husband's mind that although he painted nudes of her as an innocent young girl—Eve before she tasted the apple—and quite happily sold them on the open market, if a man so much as smiled at the real, fully clothed Sarah he was immediately suspicious. What did he say to you? What did you say to him? Did you like him? I don't want you to see him again. He seemed to think that because she was young she was easily led, malleable. *That* she had never been.

Embarrassment was the excuse she used on Roy, of course, but he knew her better than to believe it. His insistence and scoffing derision had at last worn her down. He had even gone as far as to reassure her that if she thought the finished portrait was too 'revealing' (a grin as he said it), he would arrange for a private sale through his brother, Anthony, who ran a New York art gallery and acted as his American agent.

'We shall make sure you aren't flooded with propositions from hordes of gumbooted philistines and smutty representatives of the gutter press,' Roy had boomed idiotically and won his case when Sarah had collapsed into helpless giggles. The posing had been easy, sandwiched in between various commissions Roy was working on, and now it was over the hard part had arrived. Confronting herself.

Slowly she clambered over the wall and walked diffidently into the twin of her own lounge, although this was still a working studio, strewn with canvases and paints, tins and bottles, stacks of junk and crates that doubled as furniture.

'Over here.' A shaggy red head rose from the rubble, knocking back the hot coffee with the confidence of a cast-iron constitution.

'The dramatic unveiling,' said Sarah nervously as she rounded on the covered easel. He hadn't even let her have a glimpse at the work in progress. 'Are you pleased with it?'

'It's good.' That could mean anything.

Prepared as she was, Sarah still experienced a shock of recognition, a split-second of envy eclipsed by mental rejection of the voluptuous creature in front of her. Then followed the awesome realisation that Roy was right. It was good. As good as she had feared it would be. A blending of technical skill and raw emotive power so complete that it was impossible to view the painting objectively.

The size was disconcerting to start with. Sarah felt an urge to step back to a safe distance, outside the circle of its compelling, magic spell. It was so lovely . . . the dramatic chiaroscuro and glowing colours creating an aura of seductiveness reminiscent of Renaissance paintings.

The woman—*not me, that's not who I see in the mirror every morning*—was half sitting, half lying on a bed. The background was dark and indistinct, mere glints hinting at objects concealed in the velvet blackness surrounding the shadowy frame of the brass bedstead. Warm golden flesh on the rumpled sheets in the foreground was lit by the soft yellow light from an unseen lamp.

At first glance the nakedness was explicit, but it was an illusion. The glowing light stroked the subtle contours of the body, melting away into secret shadows in a subtle portrayal of the timeless allure of woman. There was allure, too, in her expression. Though the face was not classically beautiful it had a luminous warmth and vibrance that would outlive mere beauty. She was sensuous, provocative, passionate, and the curve of the full mouth showed unashamed awareness of the fact. But it was a natural, earthy sensuality that was not too far removed from innocence.

The soft lines and curves evoked physical reality, the weight of breast and thigh, the play of muscle where the body stretched and turned, the texture of the downy skin. The hair was touched with fire as it tumbled in a disordered mane over sloping shoulders, falling to a rippling pool on the sheets. Fire slumbered too, in the wide, darkened eyes . . . inviting eyes, proud and joyfully alive.

Roy, who had been watching her face with some satisfaction, distracted her attention but not her eyes.

'Well, what do you think?'

'I don't know,' she said shakily. 'Who's it supposed to be?'

'Don't you recognise her, at all?'

'You have the likeness . . .' she had assimilated that immediately. 'But for the rest . . .'

'Not bland, pretty-pretty chocolate-box enough for you?'

'From you?' That was laughable. 'She's very . . .'

'Sexy?'

Exactly. Sarah wrinkled her nose.

'Warm? Loving? Giving?' he continued, arms folded across his barrel chest, a short, almost stumpy man whose flaming hair made such an impact that people usually didn't notice his lack of inches. 'What did you expect?'

'I don't know,' she repeated and he snorted loudly.

'What kind of artist would I be if I only painted what people wanted to see? You know the kind of work I do. I've wanted to paint you for a long time, you knew that too. Ever since I saw those of Simon's and was so sure I could do better. I had to wait until he was dead, and until you decided you were mature enough to handle what I might do with you. I'm damned if, after five years of waiting, I should have to settle for half a woman!'

Sarah looked back at the painting, surprised by his vehemence. 'But *she's* only half a woman.' The half that operated on instinct, on feeling, that half that couldn't be trusted, the half that betrayed the *self*.

'Why do you say that? She knows what she's doing and why. Which is a damned sight more than you do, you're just too damned afraid to admit it!'

He grabbed her unexpectedly by the shoulders and said fiercely: 'Look at it, Sarah, and like it. It's the best thing I've ever done. You trusted me, enough to sit for me—put yourself in my hands—so trust me now. I wasn't inhibited by living inside your skin—I could see where you wouldn't look. Look now. Be honest. You always used to be.'

He didn't wait for an answer. He strode out to the deck and vaulted over on to her side. Probably off to raid her fridge, whistling a tuneless song that told Sarah the rest was up to her. He hated explaining his art, declaring it should speak for itself to those who were willing to understand. Sarah, at last, was willing.

For too long she had been afraid, cheated on the courage and strength she had so grimly gained from living with Simon—her medals of honour, dishonoured by cowardice. She had been afraid of the woman who now looked at her with such sensual pleasure in the satisfied smile. Afraid of her power. Afraid of her vulnerability. So, like a child afraid of the dark, she had pulled the bed-clothes over her head and tried to deny the existence of the temptress. 'Don't be silly, there's nothing there' her nurse used to say when Sarah awoke in the dark in the grip of a nightmare. Nothing but herself. The most frightening and persistent fears were always the ones that came from within.

Since Simon's death her imagination had had a field-day. Her guilt that she had failed him in some way had grown all out of proportion. But what did she owe him now? Only memory, the memory of the good times. To herself she owed life, fulfilment, the realisation of her full potential as a woman and she couldn't do that by refusing to acknowledge her basic drives. She had been frustrated, angered and hurt by the limitations that Simon had tried to impose on her personality, yet here she had been, imposing even stricter limitations on herself in an ulti-mately more damaging way.

Stepping closer to the mirror-image-that-wasn't, Sarah appreciated for the first time the composed, natural de-licacy of the painted image. A woman welcoming her lover, or perhaps bidding a temporary farewell, quite unself-consciously—a moment of joyous feeling sus-pended forever.

If only such moments, such feelings were not so rare in real life. When was the last time she felt happy? Not just content but truly happy, the kind of happiness that grabbed the throat and sharpened the perceptions. It was chilling to realise that the answer was not counted in weeks or in months, but in years. She had held herself in like a tightly clenched fist . . . clutching nothing.

Be honest, Roy had said, and she was honest enough to admit that these things did not come as a blinding revela-tion. She had known for some time that her life had lost its cutting edge, that she was marking time on the brink of change, waiting for the final push that would provide the impetus to finally free her from the constraints of the past.

And Roy had given it to her—a gift of all the things that had been unsaid between them. A gift that, in spite of that first, nervous rejection, she had never seriously considered refusing to accept.

For was she, secretly, not curious? She had not allowed herself to be attracted by, or attractive to, men for fear of being trapped again in a suffocating relationship, but the thought of endless, empty, arid years stretching ahead was equally suffocating. Freedom was an internal, not external quality.

Sarah had experienced, and enjoyed, the physical side of love and knew that her body had needs that were no longer being fulfilled. Simon had been her first lover, and her last. But not *the* last . . . she had never consciously made that decision. Yet she was too intelligent and fastidious to go in for casual sex, too wary to fall in love again so soon. Perhaps the answer was merely to be *receptive*, to begin to test out those womanly instincts that had been so long ignored.

She shivered. What would it be like? she asked silently of the enigmatic painted image in front of her. To feel another man's hands upon her body? To reach out and touch, be touched? To offer herself up to the drenching sweetness of male invasion? The prospect both excited and frightened her, but she no longer feared to think it. She smiled into the dark, desirous eyes.

'Hello, Sarah,' she said.

Out on the balcony she found Roy wolfing salami, cheese and olives.

'For breakfast?'

'And last night's dinner, and lunch yesterday. I was busy. I finished the McKenzie portrait, did you see it on the other easel.'

'No.' The word spoke volumes.

'Well, it's not as good as yours anyway.' Roy grinned.

'I've decided I do like it.'

'What made you change your mind?' he asked, innocently, knowingly.

'I like it. *But* . . .'

'Ah.' He sighed. 'You're going to raise the spectre of that promise.'

'Do you mind?' The private part of her still rebelled at the thought of the public speculation the portrait would cause if shown in Auckland. Roy's work inevitably attracted a lot of publicity. If it hadn't been so . . . *good* . . .

'No.' He scrubbed some crumbles of cheese out of his beard. 'Actually I had decided to send it over to Tony when I was still halfway through. I knew it was going to be special. My market in the States is pretty strong at the moment, it'll fetch a far more inflated price there than here.'

'Mercenary beast. That's me you're blithely offering for sale.'

'Tony'll make sure you go to a good home, a very expensive home.' He rubbed his hands together and cackled. Sarah gave him a friendly thump.

'So my cowardice is doing you a favour.'

'If you were such a coward you wouldn't have sat for me in the first place.'

'The honour was too great to refuse,' she said gravely, and was amused to see the worldly Roy, used to critical acclaim, flush at her sincerity.

'Your freckles are joining up,' she said innocently and found herself bundled across to her own balcony.

'On your bike, brat, I've got work to do. Oh, by the way . . .' Sarah paused. 'My hot water heater went on the blink again last night. Can I use your bath until I get it fixed?'

'Well, get it done by a registered electrician this time,' said Sarah with a long-suffering sigh, 'not a mate's mate. And maybe you'd better stick to showers, last time I recall being locked out of my own bathroom for hours at a time while you turned yourself into a wrinkled prune.'

'But a clean prune, love, and didn't I clean the paint off the bathtub when you asked?'

'The place stank of turps for a week,' said Sarah, unmollified, and they parted with grins, Sarah lazing around until two o'clock, when she left for Julie's party feeling very light and carefree.

The Somerville's house was a low L-shaped bungalow with a lounge that opened on to a stretch of glazed quarry tiles spreading around the rectangular pool, which was screened from the neighbours' backyards by a high wooden fence.

Smoke was rising slowly into the still air from the corner barbecue as Sarah slipped in through a side gate. Most of the thirty or so people present seemed to have taken advantage of the trio of changing cubicles to strip down to bare essentials and Sarah had to pick her way over prone bodies scattered around the pool as she headed for the shade of the vine-covered pergola which jutted out from the house. Julie was there, organising drinks at the bar.

'I thought you weren't coming. Where have you been?' she demanded.

'You said any time after noon.'

'Did I? Well, you're here now. Help yourself while I farm these out.' She picked up a tray of drinks and carried them off, leaving Sarah with the distinct feeling that she had been very relieved about something.

Mindful of the heat and the way these parties stretched, Sarah contented herself with a fruit punch and moved over to watch the dying moments of a violently disorganised game of water polo. She could see Keith and Marie in the middle of the mêlée, slugging it out, and Keith's wife, Danielle, splashing around, helpless with laughter at their antics.

When the game broke up Sarah decided to take advantage of the lull and grabbed an empty cubicle, changing into a plain, streamlined one-piece bathing suit.

The water was deliciously cool on her hot skin and she swam languidly up and down the pool a few times. Though the heat of Auckland's summer sometimes palled, swimming never did and Sarah tried to do a few kilometres every day, at the beach or a local pool.

Just as she was contemplating getting out, she saw

Steven Somerville come out of the house with Max at his side. Since he had told her to use his name, she had slipped surprisingly easily into the familiarity in her mind. The verbal barrier remained as yet insurmounted.

Although Sarah had suspected he would be here today she still felt an unpleasant little shock of surprise, and floundering, nearly choked on a mouthful of water. He was wearing only brief navy swimming togs and had a towel slung over his shoulder as he stood talking with Jack a few feet from the pool. Sarah trod water, allowing herself a critical study; there was little enough to criticise.

There wasn't an ounce of spare flesh on his body and although he didn't have a tan, neither did he look unhealthily pale. His olive skin had a natural dark cast that indicated that when he did tan he would do it easily and quickly. Although he was slim he had a hard muscularity; his chest was broad with a fine smothering of dark hair which arrowed down to the flat plane of his stomach. Sarah's eyes slid over narrow hips and strong, lean thighs and she felt an odd feathering sensation inside as he changed his position slightly. He was very nearly naked and for one traitorous instant she wondered what he would look like without that brief covering.

The dark head turned casually towards the pool and Sarah hurriedly turned and swam to the far end. She didn't want him to catch her staring. Mind you, he was probably used to it. It was that arrogant assumption of his that so got on her nerves. She hoped that her new, fragile awareness of herself as a woman wasn't going to manifest itself in mentally stripping every man she looked at. Especially a man like Max, who was overpowering enough covered neck to toe! What had she hoped to discover, anyway? Some hidden defect? A beer belly or knobbly knees? Instead he was like a fined-down version of Michelangelo's 'David'.

She rested her folded arms on the edge of the pool at the deep end and sought to return her thoughts to the mundane by chatting for a few minutes with Marie, who was dangling her feet in the water and munching on a thick, juicy barbecued steak. When she got up to go and refill her paper plate Sarah was left alone and reluctantly pushed off to swim back down to where she had put her towel. Halfway she came face to face with Max doing a slow, well-disciplined crawl. She returned his pleasant greeting calmly and continued on her way, but he turned to accompany her

'I watched you from inside, you're an excellent swimmer. Do you swim a lot?'

'Quite a bit. There's a beach on my back doorstep,' she replied politely as she reached the steps.

'You're lucky.' He forestalled her intention to get out. 'I enjoy it too, but I rarely get the chance. When I do, I like to do it in style. I take my boat out on a long cruise and spend as much time under the water as on it. Have you done any scuba diving?'

Conscious of the silver drops slithering from wet sinewy shoulders through the dark curls on his chest, Sarah struggled to keep her eyes level with his. They showed an unnerving tendency to drift downwards.

'I've had the opportunity but it's never really appealed.'

'Afraid of getting out of your depth?' The familiar mockery was a relief, sparking as it did familiar annoyance. 'I suppose I shouldn't be surprised that you prefer the shallows. But you should try diving, it's quite an experience, you might even surprise yourself.'

'No thanks,' she replied tartly. 'As you just pointed out, there are all sorts of nasties lurking in the deep.'

'I'm sure a water-baby like you would have no trouble outdistancing any . . . er . . . devils from the deep,' he said, amused by her little dig. 'If you wanted to, that is. Or aren't you as confident in the water as you'd have me believe? Another false trail?'

Unsure of what he meant, Sarah frowned. Standing waist-deep in water, hair blue-black in the sun and wet face sponged of several years' age, he did not seem quite as intimidating as usual. Or perhaps it was Sarah who was not her usual self. She was seized with a sudden recklessness, a desire to beat him at his own game of *double entendre*.

'So confident that I don't feel the need to constantly prove myself. That's the prerogative of the male ego,' she drawled sweetly.

'You have a thing about the male ego, don't you?' he replied smoothly. 'How about indulging mine. A race? There and back . . . if it's not too much of an effort for you,' he added drily.

'No. But it might be for you. Are you sure you're up to it?' That seemed to strike a nerve, for the amused eyes hardened.

'I'm up to anything you can deal out,' he told her and the words were barely out of his mouth before she was off. She had no intention of giving him any advantage, fair or unfair, and thus had a fractional start. She deserved it, she told herself, for all the times he had taken unfair advantage of her, knowing she was battling to stay polite in the face of his mockery, yet still pushing, pushing until she cracked and lost her temper. He always looked triumphant when she snapped or got flustered.

She turned at the wall still ahead but he quickly moved up beside her, cutting through the water with an ease that spurred her to fresh effort. His strength was superior but Sarah was quick and light and very much in condition. She was a mere hand's touch ahead when they made the steps again and both rose up, sparkling wetly, to face each other.

There was laughter and desultory clapping from the rest of the party and a few shouts of '*viva* women's lib' and Max waved away the catcalls with a joke.

'I think she went easy on me.'

'Of course I did,' Sarah taunted, elated. Victory over him gave her fierce pleasure. 'I didn't want the male ego to suffer too much damage.'

'And provide my psychiatrist with more work? You

obviously have hidden resources, you're constantly surprising me. Congratulations,' he told her flushed, triumphant face.

'For surprising you? Or for beating you?' Sarah dared.

'Both. How many more talents are you hiding? One thing at least, that's no longer hidden—you're in excellent shape.'

He leaned slightly towards her, placing a forefinger on her shoulder and running it lightly down to the crook of her elbow. She could hardly believe her eyes when he put the finger to his mouth and tasted the water he had stroked from her arm. The lazy flicker of his tongue seemed an intimate suggestion and the look in his eyes confirmed her suspicion that he had made the gesture deliberately, to disconcert her. He did. She could almost feel the rough, moist warmth of his tongue on her skin; the sensation was indecently real and her reaction was to dash water against her arm, washing his touch away.

'And I've discovered that you're not invincible after all,' she returned quickly, ignoring a prickle of unease at his rather smug smile.

'Did you think I was?' he asked softly. 'I freely confess I'm not. But remember that I don't like to lose too often. It brings out the devil in me.' She didn't think the devil *needed* bringing out! 'Come on, come and dry off.'

'I want to stay in a bit longer,' she protested, automatically wanting the opposite to what he said.

'Really?' He looked sceptical. 'All right, I'll join you.'

For a moment they stood engaged in a silent tussle of wills before Sarah gave in. She had won, she could afford to be gracious . . . this time. She followed him out of the water and held out her hand for the towel he stooped to pick up for her. But instead of handing it over he held it against himself, just out of her reach, and stared at her body.

Sarah tensed, this wasn't an idle glance, and was fiercely glad that she had not worn a bikini. If she had looked down she would have been aghast to realise that the wet green suit revealed more to the experienced eye than even the skimpiest of bikinis. The shiny, silky fabric clung lovingly close, outlining every curve and hollow like a second skin. Although it took an almost superhuman effort she remained, hand patiently outstretched, as if she didn't give a damn that he was looking at her.

She was momentarily distracted from her agonising self-consciousness when she noticed a faint, almost imperceptible tracery of scars radiating down from underneath his left arm. They were thin and pink and quite obviously permanent. Simultaneously Sarah felt a pang of sympathy and a grim satisfaction that he was flawed, albeit it a small way.

When he moved he took her by surprise, throwing the towel around her shoulders and pulling her close.

'That suit is rather like you,' he murmured close to her ear. 'Misleadingly demure; until studied in detail.'

He held the ends of the towel more firmly, as she wriggled, then stiffened into stillness as her damp thighs brushed his hair-roughened legs. He was so close and she was electrically aware of what seemed like acres of bare skin, his and hers.

'Don't be embarrassed,' he continued smoothly, watching her blush with interest. 'You have a lovely body. You should wear less more often.'

She gasped and he let her go with a laugh. She went straight back to the cubicle where she peeled off the offending suit and used the towel roughly, externalising the tingling feeling. Wretched man! He hadn't seemed very put out at all by his defeat, considering the way he had reacted to her questioning his capability. He should have been annoyed, not amused. She could handle his annoyance, it even made her feel superior in fact, but that way he had of smiling as if at a private joke, a joke on her, was infuriating.

Sarah slipped on the underwear she had packed in the shoulder-bag and pulled the black-and-white sundress over her head. It was a simple uncrushable cotton sheath, elasticised at the waist with a slit to mid-thigh on one side. Simple but flattering the proportions of her body, which most of her other clothes failed to do. Today, for the first time in a long while she had felt the urge to wear something pretty. Now she wished she hadn't. *He* would think she was dressing to impress *him*.

She wrung out her suit over the little grate in the corner of the cubicle and tucked it into a plastic bag. Then, looping a couple of errant strands of wet hair into the dampness of her pleat, she re-emerged, thankful to have her sandals on again as protection from the blistering heat of the quarry tiles.

Over at the bar where she had left her drink Max was mixing something in a short glass. He was wearing white trousers and a slim-fitting body shirt, unbuttoned. He had been quick. No doubt he gets a lot of practice at rapid dressing, Sarah thought bitchily under cover of a smile.

He smiled too. 'I think this is the first time I've seen you out of swamp colours. What happened, did the military appropriate your wardrobe for camouflage manoeuvres? Open sandals too. My God, it's positively obscene!'

'It's my day off,' she replied, taking a firm grip on the smile.

'And mine. However there is a little matter of business we must discuss. Julie said we can use the privacy of her study.' He turned towards the open french doors, pausing with an exaggerated sigh when he realised Sarah had not moved.

'Are you waiting to be proved wrong again?'

'Pardon?' Where was Julie? Why did she get the feeling she had been manipulated yet again into an unwelcome situation?

'This is the second time you've suspected me of having designs on your virtue, isn't it? Never mind, maybe it will be third time lucky!'

CHAPTER SIX

SARAH sank into the depths of a plush leather chair and eyed Max Wilde across a large coffee table strewn with books and magazines as he did the same. He smiled, the charming smile he so rarely directed at Sarah . . . she wasn't usually worth charming.

'Well?' she asked, with wary politeness. 'What business do we have to discuss?' She was almost certain she was about to be chewed out for something.

Silently, he reached for a large black folder lying on top of the magazines, swivelling it around so that it faced Sarah.

'Open it, it won't bite,' he said, amused, as she looked at it suspiciously. 'I'd like to know what you think. Take your time.' And he settled back in his chair as she slowly did as she was bid.

It was a design folio, crammed with a collection of beautiful, bold, dashing sketches. Sarah didn't need to check the sharp, angular signature to recognise the unique style of Sir Richard Wilde.

The contents of the folder were so fascinating that for once she was able to ignore the disturbing man opposite. What a fantastic collection of clothes—feminine and elegant, practical too! As she leafed through, a pattern emerged, a co-ordination of cut, cloth and contrast which was obviously intended to extend the versatility of each basic outfit. There were suits, trousers, skirts, jackets and soft blouses to mix and match; dresses classical and timeless, dresses dramatic and different—casual yet classy, designed for living, breathing women, not just models and mannequins.

The evening clothes were rather more exotic. There was

a breath of the East in the high collars, cross-over fronts and formalised lines; the teaming of short, jutting, button-less jackets in brilliant racing-silk colours with gowns of softer hues. There were also sleek lounging suits and a more glamorous kind of mix-and-match with cobweb-fine shawls and scarves and camisole tops.

With each page were a selection of fabric samples which Sarah fingered appreciatively. They were lightweight wools and wool-blends, silks and soft, easy-fitting knits. The colours were striking and unusual combinations of muted colours with pure, clear primaries. It was not difficult to imagine the myriad ways one could combine the individual elements of the wardrobe to produce varia-tions on a theme.

'You obviously approve,' the dark chocolate voice melted into her thoughts.

'Who wouldn't?'

'You. Considering that you seem to be totally unin-terested in your own clothes. Yet you must have some fashion sense to be able to do your job properly.' He retrieved the folder and put it into a leather briefcase which he then locked and placed back on the floor by his chair. 'I thought that anything that didn't feature sack-cloth and ashes mightn't appeal to your introverted taste.'

Sarah was too curious to rise to the bait. 'Is this the Pacific Collection that there have been rumours about?'

'There's no Pacific Collection as such,' she was told. 'That's just a convenient smokescreen. What we *are* re-leasing here, and in Australia and the West Coast of the States, is a new label—*Images*. Not only a new label, a totally new market for Wilde Fashions—not couture, not mass-market, but somewhere in between.'

'What has this got to do with me?'

'Everything. I want you to model a selection of *Images* clothes for a feature in *Rags & Riches*.'

'I beg your pardon?' She must have misheard. That or he was joking in spite of his bland expression.

'Wilde's has offered Julie an exclusive on the Collection

for the April issue—it'll come out the week we hold the preview. *Rags* is going to do an eight-page feature in a 'before and after' format, aiming it specifically at the type of woman for whom *Images* is designed. Consider yourself lucky to be the chosen one.'

Lucky? Sarah stared blankly at the figure lounging in his chair. To exhibit herself in such a farce?

'It's a preposterous idea,' she said coldly. 'I've never heard anything so ridiculous in my life.'

'On the contrary,' he said calmly. 'It has many merits, not least as a good PR exercise, both for Wilde Fashions and for your magazine. And there's a more personal reason for you to give your co-operation. When the photographic session is over the clothes you model will be yours.'

Sarah opened her mouth but no sound came out. Did he seriously think that made any difference? She was familiar with the type of feature he had in mind, where a bevy of beauty experts turned an ordinary unprepossessing woman into a poised and glossy advertisement for the benefit of clothes and make-up. Done well, with style and imagination, it could be tremendously effective. Done on somebody else!

'I can think of better reasons not to,' she told him flatly. 'It's still a ridiculous idea—' She broke off and stared at his smug expression. 'It was yours, wasn't it? I should have known. No!'

'Of course it was mine. No one else would dare suggest you do something you didn't want to,' he replied drily. 'But you're perfect. I've never seen a more genuine example of "before" in my life. This feature will at least have realism on its side.'

'It's got nothing else!' snapped Sarah. 'You've made it very clear that you don't approve of the way I look. Isn't this a rather extreme and expensive method of pointing it out?'

'Cheap at the price,' he mocked. 'Since the clothes will be altered to your fitting and since Wilde's isn't in the business of selling second-hand goods, you're being offered them in lieu of payment. Although when I discussed this with Julie on Friday afternoon she did say you'd be delighted to do it for love.'

Oh did she? No wonder she had left it to him to break the news. Traitoress! That his comments were logical did nothing to soothe Sarah's ruffled spirits. Why didn't he lose *his* cool for once? He was too damned sure of himself . . . and of her eventual capitulation! But she didn't want to be reasonable. She was a woman and women were allowed to be perverse, weren't they?

'I'm not delighted and I won't do it,' she said sharply, but it had no effect. He continued to look quite unmoved. Sarah searched for something that would emphasise her distaste for the whole idea. 'And if you think I'm being coy, you're wrong! Should I feel grateful that you've condescended to play the great benefactor? Does it give you some kind of kick to think of yourself as fairy godmother to poor little Cinderella employees?'

His mouth tightened and there was a flicker of movement in the jawline that made her think that she had hit very close to the mark, but when he spoke it was with a note of boredom that was far more crushing than his anger or sarcasm.

'Don't take it so personally. I was merely pointing out the beneficial side-effects accruing from a business proposition. If you think that I have anything other than a professional interest in the matter then you grossly exaggerate your own importance. And if the idea of owning a Richard Wilde wardrobe is so unthinkable, by all means refuse it. Doubtless we can come to some other arrangement.'

Feeling like a child who has just thrown a tantrum in public—foolish and chastened—it was a moment before Sarah registered the implication of that last, throwaway line. He was still assuming her agreement a foregone conclusion.

'The question of accepting the dresses is irrelevant,

since I have no intention of modelling them,' she said, at her stubbornest. 'Find someone else.'

'Don't be in such a hurry to reject an idea you know nothing about,' he said patiently, reasonably . . . infuriatingly. 'I admit I expected some opposition from you, but I was sure that at least you would approach it with an open mind. Let me tell you something about *Images*. Then you can make your decision, and I'll abide by it.' He ignored the way she was perching on the edge of her chair, ready to leave, and rolled straight over her half-articulated protest.

'Recent market research has shown that there's a growing, untapped market here for designer fashion in the middle price range. Women want three things: a name designer, a dress that's ready-to-wear but not anonymous, and thirdly and most importantly, one that's not going to break the bank. *Images* satisfies all those criteria.

He continued, outlining the motivation behind the collection with concise rapidity, sketching the progress of *Images* from idea to reality. He made it sound dramatic, appealing and assured of success. Like himself, whispered a tiny voice in Sarah's brain.

If it had been anyone other than Max Wilde describing the idea Sarah would have applauded. But she instinctively hesitated to like anything he did.

'A "before and after" feature would strike at the heart of the market. Clothes are a confidence-builder and the aim is to show the average woman just how confidently she can wear a Wilde design. You look good, you feel good . . . it will show.'

'So why not find an average woman to model for you?' Sarah inserted.

'I have. You. You may not really be average, but you look it,' he said cryptically. 'To work, this thing has to be honest as well as dramatic, and with you it couldn't be anything but. We'll do a few paragraphs about you, have a couple of shots of you in everyday wear and let *Images* do the rest.'

'You're very confident that it will work.'

His face took on a look of hauteur. 'I am. I wouldn't help promote a line if I didn't believe in it.'

'But why me?' That sounded weak, so she tagged on: 'Why not Jane, or Nora?'

He drew a long breath, and Sarah wondered whether that spurious patience was at last running out. Would he give up?

'They already make the best of themselves, you don't. Nor do thousands of other women, women who read *Rags*. They would, if they could; if somebody showed them *how*. You're also quite photogenic—I've seen some of Mike's shots of you when you've been assisting at sessions. In fact you look better in photographs than you do in the flesh, which is another bonus.'

'Lucky me!'

'Yes, you are lucky. You have exactly what *Images* is trying to sell—potential.'

He moved his arm casually, draping it over the back of his chair so that his hand swung down, touching the folds of his open shirt. The muscles of his chest tautened and relaxed as he did so and Sarah couldn't help being acutely aware again of his body, the separate components that made up the virile whole—nerve, muscle, sinew.

He was watching her now, a faint smile on his lips, as though he guessed the effect he had on her and Sarah felt her old antagonism flare up again. She forced herself to concentrate on what he was saying, to ignore the visual stimuli.

'Most women associate high fashion with beautiful models, thin as rakes and just as human. Something that's fine to look at but never seriously considered as wearable. But basically a model's stock-in-trade is self-confidence, and the high they get from consciousness of their own attractiveness. Beauty is in the mind, not the eye—of the wearer as well as the beholder.

'I'm still not interested,' she cut in on his persuasive flow. 'You'll just have to find somebody else.'

'Aren't you being rather selfish?' He picked up the drink that he hadn't touched since he came into the room and took a pull, as though he needed it. 'You'd be helping your readers, *ergo* your magazine, *ergo* your colleagues. Not to mention yourself. Most women would give their eye-teeth to own ten Wilde creations. You're getting them for nothing.'

'I'm not most women—'

'My God, you don't have to tell me that!'

'And I'm not getting them for nothing.'

'All but.' He finished the drink, fast, then leaned back and pushed his hands into his trouser pockets, pulling the stretch fabric tight against powerful thighs.

'What is it you're afraid of, Sarah . . . besides yourself? You're not being asked to sacrifice anything. A little publicity won't turn you into public property—it'll be the clothes that are famous, not you. No one will even remember your name. And what is so embarrassingly dreadful about being made to look attractive?' Put like that the two main lines of her defence looked painfully thin.

'I just don't want to do it,' she said sullenly, unable to say why she *really* didn't want to do it. It wasn't her own importance she was in danger of exaggerating, it was his! She couldn't shrug off the fatalistic feeling that this man got whatever he wanted, regardless of what obstacles were thrown in his path.

'You mean you don't want to do it . . . for me,' he said, with uncanny perception, and his voice hardened. 'Let's take that as read, shall we? Personal considerations aside —your professional good sense should tell you it's a damned good idea. If you like the collection, and you've said you do, you can't claim you have any ethical objections.'

Sarah moistened her dry lips with her tongue, feeling herself weaken. He was right, she should put aside her dislike for him personally and consider it purely on merit.

Her hesitation finally exasperated him. 'For God's sake, what do you want me to do? Grovel?' All that sweet reasonableness was tossed out of the window when it seemed he wasn't going to get his own way after all. Grovel? She should live to see the day! 'I can't believe that even *you* are that self-centred, that humourless. Can't you even do it for a bit of fun? If you forgot about your own hangups for a moment we might get somewhere. It's not as if I'm asking you to strip off for a nude centrefold!'

The absurdity of her intransigent stand suddenly struck her and Sarah laughed, the first genuine laugh she had ever given in his presence. She laughed again when she saw the jerk of his head, the surprised expression that briefly crossed his face. What would he say if he knew she *had* stripped off? Not for a centrefold but for the artistic equivalent. That would be one in the eye for a man who thought he knew all about her just because he'd read her file!

On the heels of the comparison came another. In a way both he and Roy were offering the same thing—a chance for her to step outside herself and see how others saw her. Except Roy's assessment was based on the firm foundations of friendship, whereas the brooding man opposite, who was less of a stranger than she might wish, was dealing with superficialities. Certainly he wanted to use her for his own purposes, for his own profit, but if she accepted would she not be using him, too? A satisfying thought. And why shouldn't she? Why cut off her nose to spite her face? Deep down she really did want to wear clothes like those in the folio, spread her wings a little, explore beyond those limitations she had set herself. It was *time*. And to hell with Max Wilde and his opinion of her.

'What's so funny, all of a sudden?'

'Nothing,' she said, not quite removing the grin from her face, seeing and understanding his wariness. He didn't trust her any more than she trusted him. 'You're right, of course. When do we do it?'

'Do what?' he asked, very still.

'The feature. I agree. Isn't that what you wanted?'

He recovered himself. 'What made you change your mind?'

She shrugged, aiming for maximum annoyance. 'But I still think you would be wiser to get someone else.'

'No. You're the one who gave me the idea. You're a little on the voluptuous side for photographic modelling, but that's to our advantage in this case.' He looked her over again, but this time it was completely dispassionately and Sarah felt none of her former embarrassment. 'You've got good skin tone, and eyes and teeth . . . we may have to do something with your hair—'

'Not cut it,' she said quickly, touching the dark mass protectively. There were limits to what her newly restored sense of humour would take.

He shrugged. 'That's up to Teresa Grey, our beauty consultant. She and a fitter will be arriving on Wednesday with the dresses. The complete collection won't be sent out until just before it's to be shown.'

'Wednesday! So soon?'

'I rang the salon on Friday and gave them your measurements, plus the selection which Julie and I had chosen . . . they're probably being made up right now. Time is of the essence, I want to see the page proofs before I leave or it will mean sending them to me in London for approval—and frankly I'd prefer that not to happen. A leak at this stage of any of the designs could prove extremely costly.'

Only his first few words were important, the rest she recognised as a red herring.

'You gave them my measurements on Friday, before you'd even asked me? That was taking things for granted, wasn't it?'

'It was a calculated risk, I'm used to taking those,' he said coolly. 'Naturally I was relying heavily on your practical good sense, though sometimes you show remarkably little of it.'

Now that he had what he wanted he was prepared to be flippant. Sarah glared at him as he unfolded his graceful length from the chair and strolled over to the small french doors which opened out into a tiny courtyard at the side of the house, lined with tubs of flowering plants and ornamental trees. It was intended to be a little haven of peace but Sarah thought the clutter too studied. Her own tangle of half-wild shrubbery was much more satisfactory.

It really was unfair that the man had so much going for him, Sarah thought as Max braced himself with effortless elegance against the door jamb. It was distracting trying to carry on an argument in the face of such stunning good looks, and even more demoralising when you realised that he had the brains to match. A natural winner.

'We can do the "before" shots on Tuesday, they shouldn't take very long,' he was saying without turning his head. 'Bring in a few clothes tomorrow and we'll choose what we want. Wednesday we'll do the fittings and let Teresa take a look at you. The actual shooting will probably take three or four days, full days.'

'Well, don't expect me to shout for joy when you wave your magic wand,' she said.

'Why? Don't you want to be the belle of the ball? Have the princes paying homage at your feet? Perhaps you're the type who prefers to do the kneeling, though I can't quite see you playing the role of passive submission with any great conviction.'

She refused to acknowledge the sexual innuendo.

'I certainly wouldn't go down on my knees before *you*,' she scorned. 'I'm a little choosier.'

'More than a little, from what I can gather,' he said obliquely, then settled more comfortably against the door. 'Anyway, I can think of far more interesting places for a woman to be than at my feet. Pliancy bores me.'

'What a shame, and you must meet so much of it,' Sarah said in a breathless little-girl voice, his conceited impudence raising her hackles as usual.

He laughed. 'You forget when you smile so sweetly that you also show those needle-sharp teeth! Personally, I find the struggle between predator and prey far more stimulating than a submission without a fight.'

She walked into the trap with charming naïvety.

'The idea of man as the predator is rather dated isn't it? Women are no longer hobbled by male prejudices.' That wasn't quite true, as she had good reason to know. Several times she had been the victim of one particular male prejudice—the assumption that because she was a young widow she must be sexually frustrated, only too willing to fall into bed with a man, any man, at the mere suggestion of interest. Some of the men she had met hadn't even had the decency to wrap up their opinion in courtesy and had appeared surprised when she very firmly disabused them. She had long ago determined that peer pressure would not rule her life.

'This is the liberated half of the century,' she went on hardily. 'But perhaps at your age one does tend to live in the past.'

'I wasn't referring to *man*, little girl,' came the silky reply. 'Woman has always held the ultimate power. What chance do we poor males stand against the honeyed webs that are woven around us?'

'None, if you're weak-minded.'

Black brows arched. 'Do you think I'm weak-minded?'

'Not at all, you're still free of the silken trap, aren't you?' she retorted, rattled that she had let herself be drawn into a discussion that had crossed the borders into the personal.

'You mean marriage? So you see it as a trap, too. Was that what your marriage was?'

Her withdrawal was instant and obvious, like a snail shrinking from a probing finger.

'Was it?'

'I don't wish to discuss it.' Not when she was trying to put it all behind her. Not with him, he was far too skilful at recognising evasions.

'Why not?'

'Because it's none of your business.' Unfortunately her

adamant refusal to satisfy his curiosity only succeeded in arousing it further. She should have been off-hand, joked about it. He was such a dominant man that a sign of weakness was like a red rag to a bull.

'He was a painter, Julie said—your husband. I would like to see some of his work.'

'Why?' Sharply.

'Because art is one of my interests, a special interest. Also it might help me peel away another of your layers.'

'Why should you care?' she demanded. 'I thought I wasn't your type.'

He crushed a head of jasmine in his fist and inhaled the fragrance; not a gesture that a lesser man would have made. Much as she hated to admit it Sarah knew his sensitivity was innate, not a pose. He was genuinely perceptive and alive to the subtle variations of human response. That made him so much more dangerous as an opponent—he could follow the complexity of the feminine mind.

'My mind is always open.'

'Always? Too busy to keep union hours; you must be a success.' Something drove her on in spite of herself.

'When you get to my level, you don't have to belong to a union,' he said levelly, eyes watchful. 'And I balance my books, thank you.'

'I bet you do, you're an expert at juggling figures.'

There was an icy silence, during which he levered himself slowly upright. 'Be very careful, Sarah,' he warned softly. 'My patience isn't infinite; you are beginning to annoy me.' And then with steel unsheathed: 'Is that what all this personal antagonism is about? The fact that I enjoy the company of women and they enjoy mine?'

'That has nothing to do with it!' Even as she said it she was aware that it was a lie.

'But you do disapprove of me, that much is patently obvious. And since I don't think you can quarrel with my professional abilities, it can only be my personal conduct that doesn't meet with your impeccably high standards.'

Sarah stiffened angrily at the sarcasm. 'Just because I don't fall over myself at your charm—'

'Oh, so you admit that I have charm, we're making progress,' he sneered. 'Is it me you resent, or the sex in general? Or sex in general?'

'Don't be so disgusting—'

'So you think sex is disgusting,' he deftly twisted her words to his own purpose, looking at her with a cold, clinical interest. 'Is that what was wrong with your marriage?'

Every time she retreated he was there, baying at her heels. Now she rounded on him, fiercely.

'I told you it was none of your business. Is a woman not a woman simply because she doesn't appreciate your overblown attractions!'

'Overblown?' His thin smile held a glitter of real annoyance. 'How Victorian of you, you're the one who's out of date. Coming from a woman, and I use the term advisedly, who is so afraid of her own femininity that she deliberately de-sexes herself, I must take that as a compliment.'

The remark, with its grain of unarguable truth, flicked her on the raw and her eyes flashed green sparks of temper.

'And I should be complimented by *your* interest? I suppose I'm impressed that you get as much pleasure from dressing women up as you do from undressing them!'

The instant lift of his head was like that of a hound catching the scent of his quarry and Sarah swallowed nervously as the lean body went into fluid motion, circling slowly around in front of her, coming to a stop a few feet away.

'You really go for the jugular, don't you?' he drawled with ominous restraint. Sarah knew she should apologise but pride imprisoned her tongue. He shouldn't have started asking personal questions.

'Regretting your agreement already?' His mockery was the last straw, and Sarah took from him the one weapon with which she could strike back with impunity.

'What agreement?' she said coldly and turned to pick up her bag from the chair.

Although she had been half expecting something it was a shock to feel his hand lock around her wrist and pull her back to face him.

'You're not going back on your word,' he told her tightly.

'I didn't give you my word.'

'As near as dammit!' He jerked her so that she stumbled, nearly crying out from the pain in her wrist. Those elegant-looking hands had the strength of the devil. He looked as if he wanted to hit her almost as much as she wanted to hit him. 'I'm warning you, Sarah, don't push me.'

'Don't push you!' she exploded, her temper past flashpoint. 'How can you push a juggernaut? Why don't you just go away and leave me alone!'

'I can hardly do that now, I'm in too deep,' he said tautly, and then, considering her animated face and splendidly blazing eyes, uttered with studious insolence. 'Fascinating, you look quite vivacious for once. Want to go one further and take a swing at me?'

She had never wanted anything as much in her life! Sarah lashed out in fury, catching him on the side of the forehead with her tightly clenched fist. His hold slackened enough for her to pull away and dart towards the door, her bag forgotten.

Before she had got three steps he was there in front of her, grabbing her forearms, pinching the flesh between rigid fingers. There was a flush on the high cheekbones and for the first time she saw him fighting for control of his temper. They glared at each other until Sarah, her anger still undiminished, began to struggle.

'Let me go, you're hurting me.'

'Not half as much as I'd like to,' he ground out, tightening his grip until she whitened.

'I didn't mean to hit you,' she gasped. 'You shouldn't

have invited me to.'

'I didn't know you were going to take me up on it. Not the shatterproof Mrs Carter. Your self-control isn't what I thought it was.'

'Nor is yours. *You're hurting me.*' He didn't loosen his grip and a yellow light smouldered in the hazel eyes, promising retribution.

'Well, at least you got it out of your system. You've been dying to do that since we first met!'

'It was your fault.'

'Oh no, don't unload your neuroses on me. If you weren't so emotionally stunted you wouldn't have been so bloody hostile in the first place.'

'There's no need to swear,' she said automatically, her mind functioning on its lowest level. He had a fluent command of the language that rendered swearing obsolete and made his use of it sound doubly vicious.

'I don't suppose you ever do that, do you? You prefer foulness by implication. Very civilised of you.'

'Civilised is the last thing I'd call you!'

'Then you won't be surprised if I act the savage,' he snarled and shook her hard, until her head fell back and the predatory mouth swooped and fastened on her trembling one in a grinding, relentless travesty of a kiss.

The assault was bruising, insulting in its intensity; the pain in her arms and the soft inner surfaces of her mouth as they were crushed against her teeth excruciating. He meant to punish, to humiliate and subdue, and he succeeded. Although she clamped her mouth shut against the angry invasion she was agonisingly aware of being completely at his mercy. His strength was overpowering, never before had she been so conscious of her physical vulnerability as a woman and her mind sheered off in panic at the thought of what he could do if he chose to exercise the privilege of his strength.

She would have tried to cry out but she didn't dare open her mouth. She wanted to beg him to stop but she couldn't find the breath. He was holding her tight, so tight she could feel his heart pounding against her crushed breasts like a trip-hammer. She was helpless, she couldn't breathe, she was suffocating, she could taste blood on her tongue, she could feel . . . oh, God, she could feel . . .

As suddenly as he had swooped he lifted his head, the yellow light gone from his eyes to be replaced by one she couldn't identify. But she could identify the sudden uncoiling in the pit of her stomach, the smooth, heavy shift. Dazedly she shook her head in repudiation. How could she have felt anything but pain and fear?

'That has the distinction of being a first for me,' he murmured huskily into her confused face. 'I've never kissed a woman in anger before, at least not in genuine anger.'

Her treacherous imagination wondered briefly what dangerous, exciting love games this man might play when aroused. Perhaps he sensed the thought because his hands loosened their hold and the deep, dark pupils of his eyes seemed to expand into her mind.

'I expected you to use some of that athletic ability of yours against me.' He let his fingers trail over the marks his grip had left on her arms and felt her tremble. 'But you didn't.'

'I . . .' She hadn't even tried, she realised, just accepted his strength as superior without testing it . . . *without wanting to*. And where had her anger gone? She should be furious with him for mauling her. 'You didn't give me time . . .' she began weakly as his hands slid up to her shoulders. He smiled, an enticing, sexy smile that warmed his face from within and he pulled her towards him again, slowly, gently.

'You have time now . . .' came softly, liltingly.

The change from aggressor to seducer was so swift and complete that Sarah was bewildered, and beguiled. She had wondered, hadn't she, what it would be like to be in a man's arms again?

Curiosity warred with caution. He was no longer threatening, he was almost apologetically gentle and the

gentleness lulled her into a false sense of security. A kiss
was only a kiss, after all. Just one couldn't hurt.

She forced herself to relax as he murmured her name
coaxingly and at the first, light, restrained touch of his
firm lips her relaxation became genuine. It was strange
. . . a pleasant, cool caress, demanding nothing, nothing
but acquiescence and that was easy.

She leaned lightly against him and he let go of her
shoulders to move his hands delicately over the fabric at
her back. His skin against hers was smooth and warm, the
fresh tang of chlorine mingling with his male body smell.
He nuzzled the corner of her mouth and discovered the
tender spot where her lip had split against her teeth,
touching it with his tongue and gently sucking away the
pearly drop of blood.

'Open your mouth, darling,' he whispered seductively,
'let me taste you properly.'

Dreamily, without volition, her mouth opened beneath
his, her hands sliding up to rest on the silken shoulders
under the thin shirt. It was so warm, so enjoyable, so
pleasurable that she let herself drift in the backwash of
contentment and when the quality of their embrace began
to change she was a prisoner of her own response before
the danger even registered.

The strong, slender hands touched her neck, moved up
to her face, cupping it, positioning it so that he could
explore her mouth more freely, deepen the warm, rapid
kisses to slow, sensual ones. Her own hands slipped on the
tense muscles of his chest, fingers tangling in the dark hair
there, clenching as her body clenched with impossible
yearnings. She could no longer think, only feel, her senses
reawakened to passionate life. And as the ravishing
fantasy continued it was no longer curiosity that drove
her to arch against the virile hardness but something
more compelling, more elemental, that strove for expression.

Without knowing it she murmured his name and as he
felt her body strain against his he gave a small grunt of

satisfaction, shifting his stance and allowing his hands greater licence. They roved over her body in a journey of discovery, burning through her thin dress, describing slow, erotic circles.

His mouth roamed too, nibbling her tender ear lobes, gently biting the apple-smoothness of her shoulders left bare by her cutaway sleeves, burying itself in the sensitive arch of her throat. She shuddered as his hands slid into the small of her back, pressing hard, and she moaned into his open mouth, losing the final shreds of her reserve, feeling his tongue flickering against hers as though drinking in the sound. She had never known such darkness and heat and sweet, sweet, sensation.

How long they remained like that, fused into a sensual world bounded by each other's arms, Sarah had no idea, for time was out of joint. It was a sharp, alien sound that divided them. A door slamming and nearby voices.

He still held her by the arms, she would have fallen if he had not; but only for a moment. Then he blinked, and the wide, dark pupils narrowed again like camera shutters and he stepped back, breathing with the same shallow intensity that he had after their race in the pool. The world steadied and righted itself and Sarah was appalled by the damage done. Nothing had changed, yet everything had. Herself especially. She could feel herself shaking like a stupid schoolgirl and stuttered into stupid schoolgirl speech.

'I thought you didn't have any designs on my virtue.' Her voice was a thread of sound but he heard, and his mouth twisted.

'It's not your virtue that tempts me,' he said softly, with wry self-mockery and Sarah felt a renewed surge of heat through her body. God, what was the matter with her? She wasn't a green girl. Had she kept herself under control for too long, ready to fall like a ripe plum into the hands of the first man who kissed her? She closed here eyes in embarrassment and backed away. Even a man whom she found personally objectionable? She looked around for her bag, desperately trying to avoid looking at Max. She couldn't bear to see amusement on his face.

'What shall I tell Julie your reaction was?' he asked as her hand connected with the door handle. For one awful moment she thought he meant the kiss and spun around to regard him with apprehensive stone-grey eyes. 'To *Images*,' he added helpfully and she flushed.

'I . . . tell her you charmed me into it!' It was a lovely exit line but unfortunately she fumbled it. The door handle seemed to stick and he had to come to her aid. He didn't laugh though, he was quite kind, which to her over-sensitised mind was worse.

CHAPTER SEVEN

IF Sarah had harboured any remaining illusions that modelling was an easy, glamorous profession, working on the *Images* feature would have completely eradicated them.

After a deflatingly brief morning posing in her own clothes for the merciless eye of the camera, Sarah was hustled unceremoniously into a world of discomfort and tedium. She was made-up and made-over, pinned and poked, pushed and pulled, primped and posed. She was stared at, talked about, teased and tested, treated like an empty-headed puppet dancing obediently for anyone who pulled the strings. And of course it was Max Wilde pulling the strings.

There were compensations. The clothes were lovely, *she* looked lovely in them, and she didn't need Julie crowing over her to tell her that . . . it was self-evident. And the experience itself was interesting, if exhausting.

Teresa Grey had been an unexpected bonus. Not the glamorous, intimidating sophisticate that Sarah had dreaded, but a dizzy gamine-faced blonde prone to fits of the giggles, and given to ordering Max about with an easy familiarity that was enviable. She was also a whizz at her job and Sarah watched, fascinated, as the girl rang the changes of make-up and hairstyle, searching for precisely the right look for each *Images* ensemble—and finding it.

She had been cheerfully disgusted at Sarah's lack of interest in herself.

'You should be ashamed, letting yourself go at your age,' she had scolded on the first day, testing Sarah for colour and skin-type and pointing out all her weaknesses with professional frankness. 'I bet you've even been lazy about using cleansers and moisturisers. Now is the time to take care of your skin, before it's too late, especially if you spend a lot of time in the sun.

'You've got fantastic hair!' Her hair had surprised them all. Not even the colleagues she had worked with for three years had known of her great abundance. 'And great bone structure and you're just letting it all go to waste. Watch me and you'll get the idea . . . it's all a matter of colour and contour and balance.'

Max had been irritated that the project was taking a little longer than he had anticipated, conscious no doubt of the limited time available to him, and being the most convenient whipping-boy at hand, Sarah often felt the sharp edge of his impatience. He seemed to take little account of the fact that she wasn't a professional model and expected her to anticipate his demands before he made them—then was angry when she didn't. It was very hot in the tiny studio with the lights on and Sarah found her own temper shortening appreciably, but she tried not to let it show. She was intelligent enough to appreciate that they were all working under pressure, the pressure of time and the more subtle one of making a success of what they did, though no one really seemed to believe that Max's idea could fail—not even Sarah.

He was a perfectionist too, which made him all that much more demanding. Sarah spent endless hours hanging around, waiting for some infinitesimal lighting fault to be corrected, or listening to an incomprehensible discussion about angles, or lenses, or shutter speeds. Max revealed a technical and artistic knowledge of photography that Mike Stone, the magazine's talented photographer, was forced to respect, even to the extent of letting the other man override his professional opinion on occasions.

Sarah being an amateur among professionals, wasn't supposed to have opinions. She was just supposed to obey orders without question. And she was frustratedly aware that it amused Max to have her in a situation where she couldn't refuse or obstruct him without seeming childish and churlish; where she had to smile when he told her to, put up with being critically discussed over the top of her head as if she wasn't there, and touched . . . always he was touching her, twisting and turning her, arranging her limbs or the tilt of her head. Usually it was with a remote concentration that belied the odd physical sensations that Sarah experienced at his hands, but sometimes his fingers would linger a fraction too long, or his eyes would gleam with a knowing light as she tensed at his touch, a tacit reminder that he knew she wasn't as indifferent as she affected to be.

It was annoying, after she had expended so much effort in reassuring herself about that kiss. How it didn't matter, how it made no difference. She was convinced that her explosive response to his lovemaking had been quite normal in the circumstances. She had recognised right from the start that he had sex appeal, but her intellectual acknowledgement hadn't prepared her for the potency of the physical reality. She was, after all, a relative innocent in terms of male-female relationships, whereas he was an expert. His sensual technique had been polished with practice . . . it wasn't surprising that she should feel overwhelmed by it.

She had been naïvely curious, but his motives for kissing her that second time had been more obscure. Pique? Reflexive masculinity? Anyway, what did it matter? To ponder his reasons implied that she wanted to know, and she didn't. Far safer to dismiss it as a flash in the pan on both sides. Max was a graduate in the volatile science of body chemistry and it would be extremely unwise for a mere beginner like Sarah to start experimenting with him. At least she knew that she still had normal female reactions, she needn't worry that she had let them wither away through lack of use. And apart from anything else she still didn't *like* the man, he was too cynical, too hard, too . . . unsettling!

Even when he was being pleasant to her, it was in a backhanded sort of way.

'You're a natural,' he told her on the second morning of the 'after' shots as she stood in the small, white-painted dressing room while Teresa made a few last-minute passes with powder and hairspray. 'You don't even have to do anything. Your face isn't expressive, but it has that touch of aloofness that photographers kill for.'

Sarah looked into the mirror. The jumpsuit was silver and white with quilted, slightly pointed shoulders, a wide silver cinch belt and narrow legs. Silver threads and beads had been woven into dozens of long, thin plaits which had taken Teresa and a local hairdresser hours to do but which looked spectacular. Too spectacular for Sarah. 'I look like something from outer space.'

'Extrovert is the word I think you're looking for,' Max replied, watching her turn to see her back view. 'Agreed, it's totally different from the other clothes we've chosen but a touch of fantasy will give the sequence a lift. It may not be what you would choose yourself to wear but it symbolises the *Images* message: the way you dress can alter the way that other people perceive you, and the way that you perceive yourself.'

How do you perceive me now? Sarah wanted to ask, but prudently held her tongue. It was enough that the mirror gave her an odd sense of displacement, showing her a fantastic, wayward creature who didn't appear to give a damn about conventions. Who had never heard the word 'safe'. A dangerous perception.

'I think I like the grey best of all,' she said firmly. The dove-coloured three-piece suit in fine wool was her idea of high fashion—pencil-slim skirt, tapered trousers and pert stream-lined jacket with narrow revers.

'It suits you, I'll admit,' came the amused reply. 'A very soothing, understated elegance . . . until one receives the shock of the sexy, passionate pink blouse. Then it's diffi-cult to see anything else.' He sauntered out, leaving her wondering whether she detected wider implications in the remark.

She was instructed to leave the plaits in overnight, and a most uncomfortable night it was, too. The next day Teresa unbraided them with startling results. Sarah's hair fluffed out like a woolly pelt, floating over her shoulders in a mantle of tiny waves to complement the Pre-Raphaelite look of a thin, flowing white-tiered gown with a bodice embroidered with a glowing William Morris design.

As she stood among the masses of perfumed flowers that were to provide the backdrop for the dress, Max had come close to arrange a drift of hair so that it would not conceal the beautiful embroidery across her breasts. He took some time to do it to his satisfaction and then briefly touched the tiny corkscrew tendrils at her temples.

'Ah, yes. Perfect,' he murmured, regarding his work. Then he looked into her eyes and the abstraction on his face slipped—he smiled very faintly, making an intimate secret of it. His eyes dropped to her mouth, lingered, and came up again. A kiss by proxy. A delicious tingle shot through Sarah's body and for a moment it was as though she could feel those hard arms around her, the black head coming down to block out her vision, the warm spicy breath of him in her nostrils. It made her feel weak, lethargic, passive.

'Just relax this time. Don't try and project anything, in fact keep your mind completely blank. Let whoever looks at this picture project their own thoughts into you.' His eyes went to her mouth again. 'Open your mouth.'

'W . . . what?'

'Not that much,' he told her impatiently and she realised he was completely businesslike again. He lifted an imperious hand to her jaw and applied a controlled pressure. 'Slightly. That's right. Teresa! Could we have the gloss off her cheeks, please?'

Shakily, Sarah wished she could keep up with his rapid changes of mood. Probably he'd forgotten those enticing

words he had muttered against her lips that day. She
hadn't, and his using the same phrase had almost panicked her. She had thought he was going to kiss her again,
right then and there. She had *wanted* him to. She really had
to pull herself together!

Fortunately for her nerves, Friday was a free day. Max
and Tom flew down to Wellington to attend a national
fashion award luncheon and the shots of the last outfit, a
red evening dress, were scheduled for the following Mon-
day. The fact that the day seemed rather flat Sarah put
down to the anticlimax of nearly having finished her part
in the feature. Rattling around in the office she even found
herself looking forward to the harbour cruise that Julie
had organised for Saturday. Nothing to do with the fact
that Max would be among the twenty or so guests!

As it was she didn't see him for the first forty minutes of
the cruise, he was too busy charming all Julie's valuable
business contacts. Sarah, meanwhile, had a pleasant,
undemanding conversation with Tom at the stern rail of
the blue-and-white motor yacht.

'It's a beautiful location for a city,' he told her as they
watched the busy marina recede, framed in the background by the grey arch of the harbour bridge. 'So
unspoilt compared with many I've seen.'

As they creamed around the southern end of Rangitoto
Island past the armada of small craft, crewed it seemed by
clowns in brightly coloured life-jackets and sunhats, their
faces smeared with the ubiquitous white zinc protective
cream, Sarah listened to Tom talk about some of the
exotic places he had visited.

'Have you ever considered working abroad?'

Sarah swung around at the interjection. Max had
obviously overheard her conversation with Tom about
faraway places. He was dressed in a red-and-black striped
T-shirt and white trousers, with mirrored sunglasses
masking his eyes. He casually moved up beside them and
repeated his question about working overseas.

'Does the prospect appeal?' he pressed.

'No.' Up until now she had been too securely wrapped up in her comfortable life.

'It should. You have a good head for the publishing business, sound managerial skills. The opportunities in a country like New Zealand must be very limited; you might consider the challenges and opportunities that exist elsewhere.'

'But . . .' She raised her eyebrows at him and he looked amused.

'But what?'

'You don't usually pay me a compliment unless it has a sting in its tail.'

'I'm not paying you a compliment. I'm voicing a simple truth . . . of which you are already aware. If I was paying you a compliment I would tell you how delicious you look in that green thing.'

She glared at him, recognising the teasing inflexion. It probably stood out like a sore thumb that the stretch towelling playsuit was new. Stung into action at last by seeing the inescapable contrasts from the early proofs of the photo shots, Sarah had splurged out, buying more clothes in a week than she had in the past two years.

'I think I prefer the one about managerial skills,' she said severely, trying to ignore the fact that he had moved closer, and the long muscled forearm braced against the rail was nearly touching hers. She shifted her weight on to her other foot so that she could lean away slightly. It seemed important that he shouldn't touch her.

'Why? Because the other's too personal? We've worked quite well together this past week, I thought you might have changed your mind about not liking me. Most people like me, why not you?'

'Such arrogance,' Sarah sniped, knowing what he said was fact, not fiction . . . he wasn't given to boasting. 'I suspect you mean most *women*, and that you're talking about loving, not liking.'

Her sarcasm rebounded as he grinned rakishly. 'I don't think love has much to do with it either.'

'That doesn't altogether surprise me.'

'Because I don't debase the currency? People use the
word too freely and rarely mean it in the truest sense. If I
said I was in love with every woman I went to bed with I'd
be fickle, or a liar. If I don't say it, I'm a satyr. Either way I
can be accused of something, but personally I prefer
honesty. If ever I fall in love I'll be able to use the word in
all its pristine purity.'

'You might never use it at all at that rate,' Sarah felt
constrained to point out, though his words echoed an
answer in her heart. She too believed that love was too
precious a word to be bestowed willy-nilly on everything
from ice-cream to the deepest of human emotions. At least
a woman, if she got involved with Max Wilde, would
always know where she stood. There would be games, but
no pretence, and freedom on both sides.

'Perhaps not,' Max drawled. 'But I'm having a hell of a
time discovering what love *isn't*.'

As if to demonstrate, the rather lovely daughter of a
wool yarn manufacturer gravitated over and so obviously
hovered that Sarah was bound to introduce her. Hazel
eyes glinted briefly into grey as Max switched on the
charm. As she withdrew, Sarah suffered twin impulses
—one was to push Max overboard, the other to give the
lovely young thing a ducking! Instead she decided to take
one herself and clear her head which was fizzing with
notions of what love *wasn't* for that long-limbed devil. The
Pacific Lady had reached its destination, a private island,
owned by Julie's friends, just south of Cape Rodney.
Sarah could hear the rattle of the anchor chain, and with
any luck she would be able to experience the matchless
feeling of stepping on a shore unmarked by footprints,
human or animal.

She changed into her bikini in one of the guest cabins
and tipped the skipper a wave as she quietly swung herself
over the side and into the water. It was quite cold at first,
but invigorating, and she struck out strongly for the beach
several hundred metres away.

The small, deepwater crescent was the island's only bay, sheltered from the Gulf winds by rocky promontories at either end which formed a small natural harbour free of hazardous currents. The narrow band of white sand rose steeply to a ridge of boulders, beyond which was sandy tussock grass and the first close stands of trees. A pole house nestled in among the trees somewhere, a 'bach' the owners called it, a palatial spread was Sarah's term.

As soon as she made land, Sarah clambered over the rocky ridge to settle out of sight of the boat on the soft upward slope of grass. She lay on her back with a gusty sigh, her head in the shade of the contorted pohutukawas, letting the heat of the early afternoon roll over her. She felt her skin tighten as the sea-water evaporated, leaving tiny encrustations of salt caught in her silky-fine body hair. Wrapped in a cocoon of peace she drifted in and out of a light, refreshing doze. So warm and peaceful . . .

She awoke to a shiver of water drops and at first thought it had begun to rain, but when she opened her eyes she was dazzled. The shade of the trees had shortened and she was lying in the sun's full heat.

More droplets and she shaded her eyes and squinted at the wet figure which dropped on to the grass beside her. A brief dizziness which could have been the effects of the sun overtook her—her companion was Max.

He lay on his side and propped his head on one hand and Sarah let her own head drop back. She closed her eyes again, forcing herself to lie unmoving on her back for a few minutes more. In her imagination her already brief green bikini was shrinking further under his interested stare. At last she allowed herself to turn over casually and bury her hot face in her folded arms.

Long, long moments passed and when he laid a flat palm on her back she felt scorching shock.

'Don't.'

'You're sandy,' he said quietly, and began dusting her back. She lay rigid until his hand moved to the backs of her thighs.

'That's enough!'

His hand was removed immediately, but if anything she was even more conscious of his presence.

'You are quite the most nervous female I know. And lately you're even more tense. Did you expect me to apologise for kissing you?'

'No, of course not,' came the muffled reply. Perhaps if she buried her head in the sand . . .

'No. Not when you showed such unmistakable signs that you enjoyed it as much as I did.' And when she stayed silent. 'Didn't you?'

She shouldn't have come. She should have stayed with the crowd on board the boat. Safe. Why hadn't she? *Because you wanted him to come after you*, niggled her illogical brain. *Because you knew he would*. Not through any reasoned process, but by instinct.

'Didn't you?' He demanded with rough impatience. 'Damn you, Sarah, look at me!'

He was quite capable of forcing her to, if impatience turned to anger. Sarah rolled on to her side, putting plenty of grass between them; she couldn't meet his eyes though, and looked instead at the scarred chest.

'I meant my face, not my body,' he mocked and she flushed and stammered.

'I—I was just wondering about the scars.'

'I was in an accident,' his hand came up to stroke them lightly and the voice changed subtly, insinuatingly. 'I was in a great deal of pain for some considerable time.'

She looked at him suspiciously. The hazel eyes were wide and innocent. He was exaggerating in the hope of softening her up. The scars didn't look that bad.

'I suppose a champagne bottle exploded over you, or the lady got over-excited.'

He showed his teeth in appreciation. 'Vixen. Do *you* scratch when you get over-excited?'

Again things were moving too fast for her and she closed up. 'No. I slap faces,' she said distantly and half sat up to look over the rocks. No sign of anyone else taking to the water and the rubber outboard dinghy still rocked emptily where it had been lowered beside the yacht.

'Did he hurt you very much?'

'Who?' She tensed. Max gentle was Max devious.

'Your husband.'

She caught her breath and speared him with dark accusing eyes. 'Why are you always asking questions?'

'I'm interested. If I'm curious I ask questions. It's normal. So is answering them.'

Quite. And she would have to get over her almost pathological reluctance to talk about Simon some time. But now? With Max? It could lead to all kinds of complications. However she knew from experience that evasions only whetted Max's appetite for information.

'I just don't happen to think it matters any more,' she said with almost complete truth.

'But it does if it affects your attitude to me, to men in general. What was he like?'

'If he had lived he would have been a great painter,' she stated non-committally.

'I meant as a man,' he said, adding to her ruffled profile. 'I'm not your enemy, Sarah.'

No, nor friend neither.

'He was very—' she hesitated, how to put it into words that said not too much, but not too little? 'He was very . . . possessive.' It was a relief to say it, to relinquish another stubbornly held piece of the past. Easy, too, once said.

'Did you resent that?'

'Not at first. I was very young when we married, but it became very wearing. And painful, for both of us,' she told the rocks, the sea, the sky . . . the world.

'Jealousy is often indivisible from love, I believe,' came the remark, challenging in its very neutrality.

'He wasn't just jealous,' she turned on him fiercely, 'he was obsessive. He expected me to live through him, for him—'

'Aaah,' his sigh filled the silence as she broke off and he

lay back, his hands under his head, with a ripple of
glistening muscle across his chest. Sarah looked at his
closed eyes, the slight smile on the sensual mouth.

'Why do you say it in that tone of voice?' she asked.

'Because it explains a lot,' he said without opening his
eyes.

'What?' Sarah demanded, goaded by his reticence, for
once able to appreciate how irritating he had found her
reserve in the past.

'Why you're so scared of involvement. Why you're so
wary of men. Why you back off at the slightest sign of
interest.'

'I didn't back off at Julie's party,' she said, feeling
defensive without knowing why.

'Only because you were curious,' he said lazily. 'Did
you think I didn't know that? I'd hurt you and you
wondered what it would be like to be kissed better.' One
eye opened, catching her out in a flush. 'I hope I managed
to satisfy your curiosity.'

'Adequately,' retorted Sarah curtly and he grinned.

'You must practise these put-downs in private.' He
could read her like a book, it seemed. Both eyes now fixed
brightly on her as she plucked a blade of grass and studied
it.

'How was he killed?'

She was used to the abruptness by now, and had
discovered that an abrupt reply was the best answer.

'A plane crash.' There was an instant's stillness, then he
sat up again.

'I'm sorry.'

'You didn't know him.'

'No. But I know you.'

For some reason his gentleness upset her.

'Well, I wasn't sorry. At least not for us. For him. For
me. But not for us.'

If she had hoped to shock him she was disappointed. He
just, very softly, lifted one hand to her chin and tilted it up
towards him.

'And now? What now? Are you still sorry for yourself? Still afraid?'

She pulled her chin away, eyes sparkling greenly.

'No. And I don't need your particular brand of therapy, thank you.'

'And what brand is that?'

'Sex!' she blurted out. It was a mistake, an admission of a kind, and physical awareness snaked out to encircle them both.

'You should wait until you're asked,' he murmured mockingly, 'but would that be so awful? Sex has nothing to do with possession, not in the psychic sense—it's a sharing, giving and taking in equal measure. I have no intention of hurting you, Sarah.'

'Then leave me alone.' That smooth, creamy, coaxing voice slid insidiously along her sensitive nerves.

'Your lips say one thing, your eyes another,' he said, reaching out for her.

'You arrogant, conceited—' she gasped as an arm fastened around her waist, curving her close to him on the soft cushion of grass. His other hand came up behind the damp coronet of her hair and his mouth neared hers, lips curving, parting. Fearful . . . wanting . . . she closed her eyes and waited for the soft touch of his mouth and when it didn't come she opened her eyes again to find him grinning at her.

'See?'

Her teeth snapped shut and she wrenched herself away and scrambled to her feet. So he thought she was going to succumb easily to that practised charm! She almost made it away from him, but he was too fast for her, grabbing her ankle as she stepped out, and the result was an ignominious tumble down the slope almost to the foot of the rocks.

She was still lying, breathless, in a little sandy hollow when he reached her, placing his hands on her bare waist, holding her down, laughing openly as she hit out wildly. It was all a great game to him, he didn't care whether he was hurting her or not.

Her blows had no effect. He merely held her until at last she stopped and lay panting, glaring at him, hot and flustered by the sun and the struggle and the pressure of his hands against her ribcage. She was terribly conscious of their lack of clothing, only her two scraps of fabric and his thin blue swimming briefs between convention and nakedness. She moved restlessly, feeling the delicious languor of desire begin to weight her limbs.

Suddenly, disappointingly, he let her go and sat back on his heels. Sarah, bewildered by a sense of loss, lay staring at the thin, serious face. No trace of his former mockery remained, only a kind of tender restraint that made Sarah's heart lurch oddly.

'That was unfair of me,' he said, amazingly. 'I don't want to make you do anything that you will regret. All I want to do is kiss you . . . or rather, for you to kiss me.'

Sarah's eyes widened. Max humble? Max *asking*? She must be hallucinating! In her experience men didn't usually ask, they took first and asked later!

'I . . .' What could she say? Yes, I want to kiss you but I don't want to want to? Remembering what had happened the last time she shivered, she had gone in over her head.

Max met her uncertain gaze quite openly as she too got up on to her knees, wanting to brush the sand from herself but afraid to draw his attention to her betraying body, which still felt warm and tingly.

'Look, no hands,' he said softly, and spread his arms, palm up, out from his sides.

Was this another part of his game? Sarah, distrustful, was yet bewitched by that uncharacteristic supplication of his. Her eyes were drawn to that firm, flirtatious mouth, and she imagined renewing her acquaintance with its pleasures.

'Promise?' she murmured absently.

'Cross my heart,' was the grave reply.

Her eyes fell from his mouth to his chest, where the dark hair curled damp, now matted with sand and a few thin strands of grass. As she watched, the tenor of his breathing changed, became slower, the rise and fall of his chest acquiring a deep, hypnotic rhythm. There was a peculiar attraction in knowing that he was waiting on her, that he had placed the situation firmly in her hands. That she was in control.

Tentatively, she touched him, she couldn't help it, resting a hand just above his heart, feeling the strong, rapid beat. It was like feeling the beat of her own heart.

'Sarah?' the word was low, husky, almost strained, and she looked up. The expression on his face made her tremble inside.

Very carefully she moved closer and kissed him, very quickly and lightly on the lips and drew back. No threatening reaction, he merely knelt there, waiting. Feeling bolder, she kissed him again. Again no reaction; it was like kissing a warm statue, and just as unsatisfactory.

'What's the matter?' he asked of her frown.

'You're not helping,' she told him, piqued.

'You want me to?'

She eyed him silently.

'All you have to do is say "stop" and I'll stop,' he said and Sarah found the thought immensely liberating. In this she could trust him. He was not a boy, likely to lose his head, and he was too civilised to attempt a complete seduction here on the beach where they might be interrupted at any moment—she could hear the outboard motor spluttering to life across the calm bay. She felt safe, and she leaned forward again and put her mouth against his, a streak of pleasure shooting through her as he allowed her to coax his lips apart.

She edged closer so that the tips of her breasts brushed his chest and he began to move his tongue, slowly and erotically against the sensitive lining of her mouth. They kissed slow, sensual, heat-dugged kisses and Sarah yielded herself up to the entrancement of the moment; the fragrance of the crushed grasses, the salty tang of his lips, the soft warmth of the air all combining in a heady invitation that she had no will to resist. She would never have believed that there was such pleasure to be had from a mere kiss. Her hands stayed pressed against his chest, measuring the beat of his arousal, while his stayed obediently at his sides and yet his mouth was so skilful at enticing her enjoyment that her whole body became suffused with sensation.

'Max . . .' she sighed as the kiss was broken at last, her eyes stormy with passion, her head thrown back as she looked up at the hard-edged face above her.

'Will you let me touch you?'

Sarah nodded automatically, aching for the stroke of his hands upon her body, still trusting.

He made a soft, murmuring sound and lowered his head to hers, moving his powerful body against her in a sensuous, sinuous movement, one hand slipping in between them to cover her breast as her arms linked around his neck. At the sudden, more aggressive thrust of his tongue in her mouth, the fine tremor that shook his body, the iron-hard pressure of his thighs, Sarah dazedly took fright, alarm bells ringing frantically.

'No, stop—' was muffled against his mouth yet he instantly pulled away, or rather pushed her away, hands gripping her shoulders tightly.

'See?' he said thickly, with a crooked little smile. 'Gentle as a lamb. Putty in your hands.'

'I think that's one metaphor too many,' Sarah mumbled distractedly and his smile became more natural as he dropped his hands from her shoulders and flexed them by his side.

'We'll see. Have dinner with me tomorrow night?'

She wasn't that naïve. 'I'm tired—it's been a busy week.'

'For us all. A very quiet dinner, at a very quiet restaurant.'

'At a very quiet hotel?' she asked drily.

'The thought never crossed my mind,' he told her, looking innocently hurt. 'Julie has recommended several fine restaurants and I would like to try one in congenial company.'

'I'm sure Tom would love to go.'

'I can dine with Tom any day of the year. I want to go with you. I want to talk to you, get to know you. Haven't I just demonstrated how trustworthy I am?'

Only in the sense that he could exercise self-control when it suited him . . . to serve a purpose. She didn't doubt that he was using the verb 'know' in the Biblical sense, he wasn't proposing to give her dinner just for the intellectual pleasure of good conversation.

On the other hand, she admitted to herself, she wanted to accept the dinner invitation. Even at his most dislike-able, Max was stimulating company and her very mis-trust of his motives would protect her from the verbal seduction she was sure he would attempt. It would be a challenge, in a way, as no doubt he found her a challenge. There was no reason why she should not participate in the game, providing she obeyed her own rule: remember who he was, what he was. She would enjoy herself as an adult woman in the company of an attractive man, but she wouldn't enjoy herself *too* much. She had the rest of her life to explore relationships with men; no sense in rushing her fences simply because she had come to terms with the fact she was a woman, free to pursue her own life, her own desires, accountable to no one but herself.

'It's Sunday, there mightn't be many places open.' She made a last, half-hearted salute to the boring demands of common sense.

'We'll find one.' He held out a hand to help her up, which Sarah pointedly ignored.

He was sounding smug again, which she thought was one of his least attractive habits. So when he headed up towards the track which led to the concealed holiday home, Sarah turned and made her way back down to the water's edge, intending to swim back to the yacht forth-with. A demonstration, she hoped, that one Yes didn't concede submission. She hoped.

CHAPTER EIGHT

SARAH took more care over her appearance on Sunday evening than she had for a long time. She needed to feel sleek and well-groomed, a nice thick coat of plaster over the cracks in her confidence. Was she ready for this?

Deciding what to wear had put her in a quandary. She had not yet got around to buying evening wear and, anyway, she didn't want Max to think she was trying too hard to impress him. On the other hand she didn't think he would appreciate being seen with a woman who didn't wear her clothes well. In the end she had fossicked out her dateless 'basic black'. Simple, long and figure-hugging, it was in a silk-knit jersey, slightly gathered under the breasts, with delicate shoe-string straps.

Trying to damp down her feelings as the hour approached, Sarah wished, for the first time in her life, that she had a sister, or a close female friend, someone who could give her some sound advice on how to approach the evening. With care, of course ... but should she be off-hand, flippant, or should she try a serious appeal to Max's better nature—if he had one! Tell him that he was going too fast for her, that she was not prepared to indulge in anything more than a light flirtation? To her fevered brain even her reflection in the bedroom looked slightly sceptical. Just what *are* you prepared for, Sarah? she asked herself, and shrugged. What the hell, she would take things as they came, one at a time. For tonight she would have no past, no future, just a present. That would have been Roy's advice, if he had been here to give it.

Sarah turned off the upstairs lights and made her way carefully down the spiral staircase. The last time she had seen Roy was the previous morning, when he had bound-

ed in as she was getting ready to leave for the marina,
wanting a shower and staying on for a bacon and egg
breakfast.

'I'm taking off up north for a few days, tomorrow,' he
had told her, wolfing his food. 'Do a bit of sketching, look
up a few friends, so I shan't be monopolising the bathroom any longer. I have a guy coming in to fix the hot
water cylinder on Tuesday evening, could you let him in
for me?'

Sarah nodded. Each possessed a key to the other's front
door for just such back-scratching eventualities.

'I'm dropping you in for framing on the way,' he had
added. 'Carerra has some sort of exhibition opening at the
gallery tomorrow so it'll be a cast-iron excuse to barge in
and see if there's a free feed.' He had grinned at her brief
frown. 'Don't worry, I'll make sure he knows the rules.'

Finally, as she had dashed out the door, he had called
out slyly: 'I see life is imitating art. You'll be beating them
off with a stick in no time, darlin'.' A not-so-subtle
reference to her smartened appearance she guessed, and
he had no reason to think otherwise. She had only mentioned Max to him on the vaguest of terms, in an attempt
to prove to herself that, outside work, Max didn't matter.
And she hadn't mentioned modelling for *Images* at all. She
too had a sense of the dramatic. She would casually toss
him a copy of the April issue when it came out and enjoy
the expression on his face. Life imitating art, indeed! She
grinned; of the two men who loomed largest in her life at
this moment, each considered her transformation all their
own work.

The doorbell. It sliced through her thoughts, setting her
nerves ajitter and she brushed her trembling hands
against her dress, making herself move slowly as she
walked down the hall. Be cool, she told herself, keep your
head . . . it should be easy as long as he doesn't touch you.
Her quick tongue could defend herself against words but
her body, she had discovered, was less easy to control.

It was dusk, the summer air warm and heavy and

slightly salty. He stood in the deep indigo shadows of the large puriri tree which grew up against the house, spreading its crooked branches and glossy, evergreen crinkled leaves out over the doorstep, and Sarah's first sensation on seeing him was a faint prickle of unease. The feeling gained strength when he moved and the light from the hallway fell on to the narrow, unsmiling face. A beautiful face with a hint of ruthlessness, made even more intimidating by the impeccable formality of the black jacket and stark white shirt, the jagged edges of the black tie. The light made his eyes glow like a cat's and she had the absurd impression that he was crouched, cat-like, ready to spring.

For a moment they stared at each other and in spite of her determination to keep her head, Sarah felt a slow, disruptive charge of excitement, mingled with apprehension, shock through her. Then he smiled and the illusion of menace was dispelled.

'Something else new?' he mocked softly at the dress.

'Years old,' she told him with obvious satisfaction.

A husky laugh swirled around her. 'Unrelieved black, very dramatic. Or is it supposed to indicate mourning?'

Only Max could ask such a question. 'Ask me that in a few hours time,' Sarah fenced and he laughed again and extended a flat hand, revealing a flash of silver at his cuff.

To avoid having to touch him Sarah turned and made a business of shutting the door and checking the lock, transferring her clutch-bag to the hand nearest him. When she faced him again his arm was back at his side and he merely stood back for her to precede him to the car, an ironic twist to his mouth.

He settled her in the passenger's seat, then slid behind the wheel and started the engine, backing out with swift economy of movement and accelerating smoothly away from the curb. He seemed preoccupied by more than just his driving and apart from a few remarks about the car, a hired BMW, and a request for directions, was silent on the drive. At least it was not a stiff, awkward silence, Sarah consoled herself.

She was not surprised when they drew up outside one of Auckland's most prestigious, and expensive, restaurants . . . only the best for Max, always. *So what are you doing here, Sarah?* Why did he give her this inferiority complex?

The two-storeyed wooden building had originally been a family home, on the grand old Edwardian style and the atmosphere of a gracious upper-class residence had been retained in the conversion. They were shown, by a deferential *maître d'hôtel*, to a table outside on the verandah, screened from public view by a trellis of vines which grew from balustrade to eaves along its length. Enclosed lanterns at each table provided the soft lighting.

It wasn't until they were seated, waiting for the wine steward to return with pre-dinner drinks, that Max looked at her fully again, with an odd intensity.

'I don't think we said hello, did we?' She was the focus of a magnetically attractive smile. 'Hello, Sarah.'

'Hello . . .' She was annoyed at the breathlessness of her reply.

'Still stumbling over my name? Do you realise that the only time you use it easily is when you're in my arms.' He paused, musingly. 'I suppose I shouldn't object if you choose to make my name an endearment.'

She avoided his teasing eyes. This was another man again, a relaxed, almost whimsical one without that careful control that had seemed such an intrinsic part of his personality. Consequently, he looked younger, less jaded, more dangerously attractive than ever.

'Black suits you,' he continued, appraising her further. 'A pity there wasn't something black for *Images*.' He leaned back slightly to allow the wine steward to place their drinks on the table. 'Although what we have is quite sufficient—more than sufficient. It's shaping so well that the feature may be syndicated to other Wilde publications.'

Sarah wasn't sure she liked that idea and her doubt

must have shown for he said, with mild exasperation: 'Don't tell me you haven't considered the possibility, it was always on the cards. You're not going to turn coy now, it won't wash, in view of—'

'In view of what?' she asked, when he stopped and took a pull at his Martini.

'The fact that you've enjoyed yourself on this assignment,' he continued smoothly after the tiniest of hesitations. 'Barring minor . . . er . . . differences of opinion, that is. What do you think of the proofs?'

Sarah shrugged. 'They're excellent.' But he didn't need her to tell him that.

He made a derisive sound. 'No self-congratulations? Don't you possess any vanity at all?'

'As much as anyone, I suppose.'

'No, you don't.' The hazel eyes gave her a curiously baffled look. 'You frequently walk past a mirror without even a glance . . . even when you're wearing my father's best efforts. You never touch your hair, or make any of the subconscious gestures a woman makes to check her appearance. I can't believe that you're so genuinely unaware of the effect you're creating.'

'What effect is that?'

'It's not necessarily a strength you know,' he said, ignoring her question. 'A small dose of vanity or envy would round off some of those edges that other people bark their shins upon.'

'Is that what you prescribe. A teaspoon of the seven deadly sins?' said Sarah lightly.

'Perhaps not all seven . . . but I think I've made myself clear on that subject before.'

'Crystal. You have a winning way with an insult,' Sarah told him, a trifle tartly.

'Learned at my mother's knee.'

Sarah's over-sensitised ears detected a hint of underlying bitterness in the smooth reply. Was he speaking the literal truth? Was this another tiny splinter of vulnerability threatening to work its way under her skin? She resisted it, remembering how skilled he was at manipulating people.

'You're lucky,' she replied. 'The only things I learned at my mother's knee were already thousands of years old. I decided not to embark on a course of continuing education, whereas *you* . . .'

'Now, now,' he admonished, with a gleam of appreciation, 'no fighting tonight. Shall we declare a truce?'

Sarah took a cautious taste of her sherry. She had better be careful, she didn't have much of a head for alcohol.

'Sometimes I can't help it,' she confessed.

'I know what you mean,' he murmured. Thick, dark lashes lay briefly against his skin as he looked down, idly stirring his Martini with the olive on a toothpick. Then the lashes swept back revealing the large dark pupils ringed by a halo of hazel. 'Why do you never wear any jewellery?'

'I . . . I don't own much.'

'Except your wedding ring.'

Sarah looked down at her left hand. 'That's an heirloom. It belonged to Simon's grandmother.'

'No engagement ring?'

She was past resenting his inquisitiveness. Besides, by answering some of his questions yesterday she had given him tacit approval to ask more. 'We didn't have a formal engagement. And anyway, Simon didn't believe in over-adornment, or in acquiring possessions for the sake of it.'

'Except you.'

Sarah's fingers curled into her palms at the quiet irony. 'That's not quite fair,' she protested, equally quietly. 'There was more between Simon and me than . . . perhaps I shouldn't have said what I did yesterday.'

'Why not? Who was it who said that one owes respect to the living; to the dead one owes only the truth?'

'Voltaire,' replied Sarah automatically, having come across the quotation in her extensive reading after Simon's death, when she was trying to come to grips with her feelings about grief and guilt and the resulting emotional mess.

The man across from her smiled. He was too clever by half. Sarah gave him her haughty look.

'You should wear jewellery—gold perhaps, something warm and yellow, or rich and red, like rubies,' he said, to punish her, his eyes drifting over her bare ears and throat, to the beat of the pulse above her collarbone. 'But perhaps you're right,' he continued provocatively, 'bareness makes its own statement . . . and it's often a more interesting one!' His eyes dropped lower and glinted with satisfaction as she hastily brought her arms up on to the table in front of her, resting her chin on her hands, shielding the warm swell of her breasts from his gaze.

Sarah felt herself flush with a mixture of embarrassment and annoyance. Damn him for a disturbing devil! She had worn the dress braless before and not felt self-conscious, yet he made her feel a brazen hussy. In fact she had tried a strapless bra under the dress this afternoon, but the lace had been bulkily obvious under the thin silk and she had stuffed it back into her drawer, feeling a coward for having tried it on at all.

'Calm down, Sarah,' he said mockingly. 'I'm not going to leap on you in the middle of the restaurant. Credit me with a little finesse.'

'Oh, I credit you with more than a little,' she managed sarcastically, 'and it's not exactly a calming thought.'

'I'm glad you find it exciting,' he said, wilfully misunderstanding her and then disconcerted her by changing the subject. 'I meant what I said about your working overseas. Why don't you consider it? London perhaps? Wilde's has several publishing concerns there. I could make some enquiries if you like.'

'I already work for Wilde's,' she said, not sure whether he was serious or whether it was just part of his line.

'You're being obtuse,' was all he said.

'Still intent on playing the fairy godmother?' she taunted, deciding to take him lightly, fearing to do anything else.

His mouth turned down at the corners. 'I admit that at

the time you accused me of being condescending my attitude may have been rather patronising, but I've since been cured of that. I suspect that Cinderella possesses more than enough of her own brand of magic.'

And with that enigmatic utterance he turned his attention to the listings in the leather folder beside his plate, and suggested that she choose from the menu for them both.

'Tom told me that cooking is one of your hobbies.' Sarah had a momentary frisson at that, remembering the other things she had told Tom during their numerous conversations. 'Well, wine is one of mine, so let's collaborate.' And, drily: 'Your surprise is most unflattering. I know I open car doors for women but that doesn't mean I'm the complete chauvinist pig. Have I ever given you reason to think that I was?'

In truth, he hadn't. He was quite prepared to meet a woman on her own intellectual level, whatever it was, and certainly showed no signs of treating them as second-class citizens. And, Sarah realised with a flash of wisdom, he was confident enough of his own masculinity not to have to reinforce it by acting the macho male.

Together they decided on champagne to accompany the first course of smoked roe pâté and vichyssoise soup and with the main course of chateaubriand a distinguished French red. Both agreed that dessert would be superfluous.

As the conversation flowed easily back and forth, Sarah relaxed enough to enjoy herself. She was seeing yet another facet of this most complex of men, a fascinating one. Max was cultured, witty without effort, mining a rich vein of humour which abhored posturing and pretentiousness. They discussed books and music, people and current events, exploring mutual ground and areas of irreconcilable difference alike, sometimes earnestly, sometimes humorously. Yet Sarah was ever aware of the undercurrents to the conversation and whenever she seemed in danger of forgetting the fact that they were man and woman, Max would re-introduce that note of seductive intimacy to which she was increasingly vulnerable.

'I'm glad Teresa gave you a fringe,' he said suddenly, in the middle of a discussion about New Zealand wines. 'It means you can't hide your hair away any more, even when you scrape it back as you have done tonight. Is that piece of not-so-subtle body language directed at me?'

'I always wear it up,' Sarah said, put off her stride.

'Not always, surely,' he murmured.

'I sometimes wear it loose at home.'

'In bed?'

'Yes, I mean, no,' stammered Sarah. It was amazing how evocative a couple of words in those chocolate-flavoured tones could be. It raised all sorts of images between them. 'I usually plait it at night, otherwise it gets very tangled.'

'I imagine it would, but it would be a pleasure to untangle,' he said softly over the narrow rim of his champagne glass. 'Does confining it so strictly during the day enhance the nightly private pleasure of letting it loose?'

Sarah's mouth went dry. 'You make it sound almost wicked,' she said faintly.

'It is wicked, a wicked waste.' He finished his creamy, chilled leek and potato soup and rested his chin on linked fingers, as he often did when thinking. Sarah concentrated on her pâté, her face a serene mask while her heart skipped erratically, waiting . . . waiting . . .

Yet again he indulged in a verbal retreat, leaving her poised on the edge of frustration. When was he going to put into words what was in both their minds, so that she could get her little rehearsed refusal over and done with? This time he was talking about Sir Richard, describing his working habits with a mixture of respect and unfilial sarcasm.

'He sounds rather formidable,' Sarah commented. 'I should be in a constant state of terror if I had to work for him.'

He looked amused. 'People call me formidable, but you're not scared of me . . . quite the reverse.'

'Perhaps they mean *formidable*,' said Sarah, giving the word its French pronunciation.

'Is that a compliment?' he pounced.

'From me? Never!' Sarah hid her smile in her second glass of champagne. The heady brew was so fine and light and dry that it almost crackled in her mouth. She felt she could drink it all night and not be affected.

'Never say never, Sarah, that's tempting fate. I'll get a good word from you yet.'

'I think you have a surfeit of those already.'

'Not from you. But I can wait.'

'Somehow I get the impression that you're not very good at that.'

'I'm learning,' he said, with wry self-mockery. 'You like getting your own way almost as much as I do. You'd have made a good schoolmarm . . . or mother. Were you and your husband planning children?'

Sarah shook her head abruptly.

'Don't you want to have children?' He sounded vaguely shocked.

'Your chauvinism is showing,' she told him with a trace of the schoolmarm. 'But yes, I do; some time.'

'Then it was your husband who didn't.'

Recognising the relentless look on his face Sarah gave in gracefully. It no longer had the power to hurt her, anyway. 'Simon was the child in our marriage,' she said candidly. 'Or rather, his talent was.'

'My God, it seems to me that you got precious little out of that marriage,' he said, with what she thought was unnecessary harshness.

'I got myself. I grew up. I learned about art, and beauty and truth, and about love,' she smiled wistfully.

'And where have you put all this education to use?' he asked brutally. 'How many men have you been out with, like this, since Simon died?'

'A few.' To relieve the intensity of their conversation

Sarah made a bright joke about some of her matchmaking editor's pushier candidates, but it fell flat and Max muttered something under his breath. 'What did you say?'

'I said—clumsy idiots.'

'My clumsiness as much as anything,' Sarah admitted. 'I went out with them for all the wrong reasons. At that stage I wasn't ready to make any kind of concession to any man.'

'But now you're ready to experiment a little,' he said, deceptively casual.

Her reply was too quick, too emphatic. 'No. No. Not at all.'

'Liar,' he challenged and she stilled, like an animal cornered. Max's steady eyes were almost straw-coloured in the lamplight—the colour of the champagne in her glass. Champagne eyes and champagne, they both beckoned her to recklessness.

In a moment she was lost, her own honesty defeating her, at last giving in to the strength of the attraction he held for her. She had tried to avoid it, been careful to nurture dislike, explaining away the tension that she felt in his presence as antagonism. But it wasn't. It was more complex than that, and more simple. It was sexual tension, and she felt it enveloping her now, prickling across her body like a rash. She lowered her lids, flustered, and lifted them again. He was still watching her, with a virile certainty that was intoxicating; he was way ahead of her, on all counts. He knew she wanted him, he wanted her—the desire in his eyes no longer veiled, but burning a steady flame. Sarah didn't want to fight him, or herself, any more. There was a sense of inevitability about it, as though every encounter, since their first meeting, had been leading up to this. Deep within her the battle had been fought and lost some time before; only her timidity, her fear of the unknown depths of her own passion, had prevented her from admitting it.

The searing moment of mutual recognition was interrupted by the waiter, who took their silence as a cue to offer a few pleasantries, cleared the table and re-laid for the main course. The red wine was delivered, opened, tasted and poured, and the chateaubriand, a tender, succulent fillet of beef, crusty brown on the outside and meltingly pink at the centre, arrived on a silver salver surrounded by an array of crisp-tender vegetables.

Max calmly began to eat while Sarah wondered where her appetite had gone, and tried to ignore the pangs of a more urgent hunger.

'Eat. It's good,' she was told, and Max smiled approvingly as she obediently picked at her food.

'What a good child you are when you're not arguing.'

'I'm not a child.'

'You are in some things,' he said, supremely confident. 'You don't know very much about men. About the way they think and act, about how they feel in relationship to you. Don't you know that coolness and disinterest is a challenge to any man's masculinity?'

'Is that all I am to you, a challenge?'

His smile glittered at the note of chagrin. 'Mere challenge I can resist; mystery is something else. The question is, what am I to you?'

That was a question Sarah didn't even want to consider.

'A challenge, perhaps,' she murmured, trying for archness and achieving mockery.

His eyes narrowed. 'Perhaps you do know. Perhaps this nervous apprehension is just a pose.'

She didn't pretend to misunderstand. 'I loved Simon. I never looked at another man while he was alive, and afterwards I never wanted to.' Then she felt embarrassed at the blatancy of her statement, but Max simply nodded and began to draw an intricate pattern with his fork on the white linen table-cloth. A lock of straight black hair fell forward over his brow and he was frowning slightly with concentration. Sarah longed to lean over and make contact, sooth out those furrows, make him look at her again with that warm, sensuous gaze.

'What about friends? People you knew before and during your marriage . . . other artists?'

'I more or less lost touch with them all,' she said meekly. 'Quite a few of Simon's so-called friends were just hitching a ride on his reputation. After he had gone we had no common interest any more.'

The pattern became even more intricate. 'All of them. You have no contacts in the art world now?'

'Acquaintances. Except—' she paused, fascinated by the convoluted wanderings of the fork, and the fork paused also.

'Except?'

'I have one friend, a painter . . . I owe him a lot.'

'You have a close relationship?'

'Not the kind you're implying.'

'No romance?' He seemed to tire of his game, throwing down the implement and stretching his shoulders back against his chair. He sounded vaguely triumphant, Sarah thought, annoyed. It was a bit late now, asking whether she was involved elsewhere, when he had already made his dishonourable intentions clear.

'No romance,' she repeated neutrally.

'What about before Simon came on the scene?'

'Do you want the story of my life?' she asked, exasperated, and sighed when he nodded. 'No, there was no one before Simon.'

'Just establishing precedence,' he mocked. 'So there's only been one man in your life, and he put you to sleep. It's about time you were woken up.'

'Have we swopped fairy-tales now?' Oddly enough she did feel as if she had woken from a long sleep—dazed and heavy, and filled with languid longings. She used her cutlery slowly, deliberately, aware of the eyes on her mouth as she ate, making of it a sensuous act. The rich white *béarnaise* sauce was redolent of tarragon and chives, which she would forever after associate with this meal . . .

this man. She sipped her wine, and the ruby liquid left her mouth warm and red.

'I think we're going to create a tale all of our own,' he replied. He seemed on the verge of saying more, but restrained himself. At times this evening he had seemed almost hesitant, as if pondering the consequences of what he was doing, and at others he had given her potent reminders that he was not a man to give up easily, if at all, once his mind was made up.

Sarah waited until their plates had been removed before bursting out with: 'This is absurd, I hardly know you!'

'That's the way it takes you, sometimes.' He declined coffee with a brief gesture of his head while a steaming cup was set in front of Sarah. 'But if you want to know anything, ask—I can't guarantee that you will like the answers you get, but they'll be honest answers.'

Sarah opened her mouth and shut it again, and laughed ruefully. 'I can't think of a question now, not when you're looking at me like that.'

'Is this better?' He dutifully averted his eyes, chin on hand, to study the ornate silver salt-cellar on their table. It was; relieved of the searching intensity of his gaze Sarah found her tongue, and asked, her interest stimulated by their earlier conversation:

'Are you and your father very close?'

The slender fingers stilled on the scrolled silverwork and his lowered lashes flickered. She knew he had been expecting a question about past love affairs, or whether his rakish reputation was earned, but strangely neither really mattered to Sarah any more. She was with him now, and that was enough. But she *was* interested in what made him tick as a person—what motivated his singular drive. 'You can look at me now,' she told him blandly.

'You make a career of being unexpected, don't you?' he told her and linked his hands as he applied himself to satisfying her curiosity. 'No, my father and I are not close.

We're too alike in some ways to get on well, in others we're too different.'

'How different?' she prodded, pleased to be the examiner for once.

'He believes talent and temperament are inseparable. I don't. I believe that self-discipline enhances and concentrates a talent, in whatever field. My father does everything to excess, except parenting. He had a distinct lack of talent in that area, as did my mother.'

'So you don't live together?'

'God no!' He looked appalled at the very thought. 'We deal very well together at a distance. In spite of his failings as a father, or perhaps because of them, he seems to be developing a compulsive need to meddle in my life—both personal and business—and refuses to concede that I am more than capable of dealing with my own problems.'

'A fairly common complaint among sons, I would imagine,' said Sarah, amused by the aggrieved note in his voice, and wondering what specific remembrance had induced it.

'Perhaps,' he allowed. 'But I have achieved my present position with very little help from him—' He saw her scepticism. 'It's true, intentionally or unintentionally he made things very difficult for me during my formative years with the company. Perhaps he feared that one day I would push him out.'

'And would you?'

A faint smile. 'No. I think that has been proved beyond doubt.'

'What do you mean?' she asked curiously.

He seemed to give himself a mental shake. 'I mean I recently discovered that I have no wish to crush the old man, even if it's in my power to do so. He may infuriate me, but he is my father, and a designer of undisputed genius.'

'Is that why you didn't become a designer? Because you didn't want to compete with him on his own ground?' asked Sarah with sudden insight.

'No, I—' He stopped, and a brief expression of confusion passed over his face. 'At least I don't think so, I've never been interested in designing—'

'That doesn't answer the question.'

'No, it doesn't, does it?' She saw him smile and erect the 'no entry' sign. 'I think this conversation is getting a little . . . involved.'

'You didn't say that when I was the one under the microscope,' Sarah accused, not wanting to let him off the hook so easily.

'You're a more interesting specimen than I,' he told her, with adroit insincerity and she had to laugh.

'How clever you are at evasion.'

'Almost as clever as you,' he agreed smoothly, and Sarah felt a small spurt of rebelliousness.

'Are you secretly insecure?' she taunted. 'Is that why you never let your women get too close to you?'

Black brows rose. 'We haven't established yet whether you are one of "my women".'

Sarah glared at him and his mouth twitched temptingly.

'It is commonly known that you like to flirt. That your attitude to your . . . to female companionship is easy come, easy go,' she said, and felt ridiculous as he clicked his tongue.

'Sarah, Sarah,' he said, with mock-disappointment. 'You've been reading the newspapers again. Who are you going to believe, them or your own instincts?'

'Both, they both tell me the same thing!'

The hazel eyes gleamed with pleasure and laughter as he leaned forward in a confiding manner and Sarah instinctively leaned forward also.

'Do you know what the dictionary definition of "flirt" is?' His face was disconcertingly close and as she watched the words form on his lips she was swamped by a sudden surge of desire. She wanted to pull his head even closer, run her fingers through that silky black hair, feel the movements of that mobile mouth against hers. The feeling was so intense that she had difficulty controlling it, and grasped her hands tightly in her lap to prevent them betraying her by reaching out for him.

' "To pretend to make love",' he quoted softly, insinuatingly. 'I don't qualify, Sarah. I don't *pretend*.'

'You told me you didn't use the word "love",' said Sarah, her voice husky, eyes fixed on his face, inextricably caught in a web partly of her own making.

'I'm not talking about emotion. As the description of a physical act the word is very apt. When I go to bed with a woman we don't just "have sex", we engage in a mutual ravishment of the senses. Purely physical gratification doesn't require a partner—but to make love . . .'

Sarah felt her skin bloom with colour and struggled to overcome what seemed to be an acute lack of oxygen. Her breasts rose and fell quickly as she began to breathe rapidly to make up the deficiency. She could not have felt more flustered if he had suited his actions to his words.

'Does that frighten you?' He seemed to be flattered by the idea, so that she would have liked to deny it, but she didn't.

'Yes.' It was like being on a high board, wanting to feel the exhilaration of the dive, and aware that fear played a part in that exhilaration.

'But it excites you, too,' he read her perfectly. 'As you excite me.' He moved in for the kill, catching the hand that came up as though to fend him off. 'But it's more than purely physical, Sarah. I like your mind, I admire your independence . . . I understand it, we're two of a kind in that respect.'

In the midst of the toils of desire, Sarah denied that. 'I want to be free because I know what it's like to be a prisoner. You want me to be free because it absolves you from any kind of responsibility, because an independent woman won't clutter you up with emotional demands.'

'Isn't that the pot calling the kettle black?' Max said drily, the banked fires still visible in his guarded eyes. She was aware that he was stepping delicately and she couldn't blame him. It had been a stupid thing to say, because she was going into this thing with eyes wide open, as selfishly as he was. She too was scared of emotional clutter. Desire without responsibility, that was what she wanted.

'Don't you want us to meet as equals?' he asked, and suddenly she found her answer, looking at her hand enveloped in his.

'No.' His face altered, though he masked his uncertainty well, and Sarah smiled, putting all the feeling she could into the lazy invitation in her darkening eyes. 'I don't want to be an equal partner—' she paused, deliberately heightening the tension between them—'I want to be seduced, I've never been seduced before. What's it like?'

There was an incredulous silence. Then he laughed abruptly, with as much frustration as humour. 'Just when I think I'm beginning to work you out—! My God, that's another first . . . I've never been asked to seduce a woman before, at least not in words. I begin to wonder who is seducing whom.' He gave her a long, slow look—her eyes, her mouth, her bare shoulders, the golden promise of her breasts. 'But I accept the invitation, of course, how could I refuse without ruining my reputation?' Now both of his hands held her submissive one. 'You're so elusive that even the colour of your eyes shifts. They're dark, almost purple at the moment. What colour will they be when you're aroused, I wonder? Or are you aroused already?' The last word slurred to almost a whisper and one hand slid to her wrist. Her pulse beat hard and fast against his thumb and she could feel a slight ridge of hardened flesh on his palm. Another scar? Soon she would feel it on the soft skin of her body and she went weak with imagining it.

With slow deliberation he brought her hand up to his mouth, palm upwards and bit gently, voluptuously into the soft base of her thumb. It was a statement of sexual power and Sarah's eyes half closed as she felt a deep, molten flowering inside her, her body softening in a way that made the man across from her catch his breath.

She was hardly aware of leaving the restaurant, or of the journey home. Only of Max beside her, controlling the powerful car with ease, glancing sideways every now and then with barely concealed impatience.

He followed her up the darkened stairwell to the studio where she had left a single, soft orange lamp burning. She kicked off her shoes and floated over the polished wood floor towards the light, like a moth drawn inexorably towards the flame.

CHAPTER NINE

THE dark volume of the night pressed against the wide expanse of uncurtained window; cloud hung like smoke across the thin, pale face of the moon. There was no wind, not a sound but the chorus of crickets outside in the darkness, no witness but the large, soft moths beating their wings against the glass, drawn like Sarah to the spell of the light.

She was trembling. Here in familiar surroundings what had seemed so inevitable now seemed less certain.

She heard a soft footfall, felt hands descend lightly on to her shoulders.

'Have you changed your mind?' There was a thread of amusement in the voice that caressed her ear. He knew so much about women, he must know what she was feeling. 'If you have, tell me, this is supposed to be seduction, not rape.'

He turned her slowly around and she stared hard at the black tie, sensing rather than seeing his mouth curve.

'Shy, mistress? You wanted me to take the first step and I have. All you have to do is say yes.' His hand tipped her chin up and held it until her eyes lifted to meet his. What she saw there made her tremble anew. 'Say yes, Sarah,' he urged softly. 'Say yes. I won't hurt you. I promise.'

Without really being aware of it she allowed her body to sway, drawn by the magnet of his. Her voice held a question as well as an answer.

'Max? . . . I . . .'

It was enough. One lean, dark hand slid around to the back of her head, gripping her firmly, pulling her forward. He bent and brushed his open mouth tantalisingly across hers, drawing back as she stirred and tensed like a warm, wild animal in his arms.

'Relax. Don't be frightened,' he soothed.

'I'm not, it's just . . .' Sarah gasped as he nuzzled her neck, finding with his tongue the throbbing pulse at the base of her throat. 'I don't remember—ever—feeling like this.' The words slowed and slurred as she threw back her head to allow his mouth access to the sensitive skin just under the curve of her jawline.

'You never have,' he muttered against her with sensuous satisfaction. 'Nor have I. We're a unique combination and the way we feel and fit together will be unique too. I want to pleasure you and show you ways to pleasure me . . . we have all the time in the world . . . we can take it slowly, gently . . .'

He was keeping a tight rein on his passion and Sarah rebelled. She was a woman and wanted to be treated like one. She didn't want restraint, she wanted Max as she sensed he could be—fierce, passionate, volcanic—excitingly male. The driving need inside her would be content with nothing less.

She freed her hands, crushed between her body and his and held his head, stilling it. The hard shape of his skull in her hands was strangely affecting. Such fire and strength and intelligence inhabited that delicate structure. Such a man. Her eyes widened, showing him dilated pupils almost swallowing the violet-shadowed irises.

'Not too gentle, I hope.' Her bewitching dismay died under the ravishment of his lips. She made a soft, contented sound and his mouth hardened, deepening its erotic penetration. The darkness grew in around them, the orange pool of light like a glowing bubble of sexual tension enveloping them, isolating them.

Sarah stretched her arms and wound them around his neck, leaning into him on tip-toes, closing her eyes and drinking him like an intoxicating draught. She felt his hands move on her head, then the weight of her hair began to shift and she realised what he had done. Her head

jerked back and he let her go, watching as she moved out
of his arms and raised shaking hands to struggle with the
unanchored pins.

'Let it down,' he ordered thickly. 'I want to see it down
around you, I want to hold it in my hands.'

Impatiently she shook her head to release the knot and
the heavy, luminous mass fell down. She heard a sharp
hiss of indrawn breath as Max stared, following with his
eyes the rich, rippling glow as it veiled the curves of her
body. He had seen her with her hair down before, in the
studio, but now he was looking at her as if he had never
seen her before, the expression on his face fascinated,
absorbed. For the first time in her life Sarah felt a true
sense of feminine power.

As the seconds ticked by the tableau remained, Sarah as
fascinated by Max as he was by her. He stood as if
transfixed, feet slightly astride, hands hanging loosely at
his sides, breathing slowly and deeply, eyes half-closed,
face drawn tight, nostrils flared. He looked magnificent,
savage, stripped of all that elegant charm that masked the
elemental man. And in Sarah the elemental woman was
fired in response.

Provocatively she turned her back on him, finding the
last of the pins and drawing them out of her hair, placing
them on the table beside the lamp. Then she began
running her fingers through the tresses, pretending she
had forgotten the man behind her.

He moved at last, with sudden violence, pulling her
back against him so that she felt the hard muscularity,
sliding his hands around her waist, splaying long fingers
over her stomach as he buried his face in the scented
curtain at her nape.

'I've run you to earth at last, little vixen,' he growled.
'There's no escaping me now; no laying of false trails or
doubling back. Just you, and me, and this.' He moved his
body deliberately against her so that its heat penetrated to
her very bones, turned them soft with exquisite anticipation. She tried to twist around in his arms, but he

wouldn't let her, hands tightening over her hip bones, tangling in the fine ends of her hair.

'Don't be so impatient,' he tantalised, a warm, exultant note of laughter in his voice. 'You must earn your satisfaction. I promise you, my wanton innocent, the pleasure will be all the more intense for it. Relax. Enjoy what I'm going to do to you.'

There was nothing she could do but obey, arching towards his hands with a sigh as they slid up to cup the aching fullness of her breasts, his thumbs brushing teasingly over the hardening tips. Her head fell back on to his shoulder, her safe, ordinary world exploding into a rapturous excitement of the senses beyond anything she had ever known. A stinging desire that streaked along her skin and nerves until her whole body was afire with it. At last, when she thought she could bear the slow, tormenting caresses no longer he turned her closely in his arms, the hardened contours of his body evidence of his own arousal.

He kissed her eyes and nose and mouth, and her hair where it waved thickly over her ears, and lifted his head to look at her dreamy face, touching her dark tresses.

'I know now why you keep it hidden. Like this it's too much of a temptation. Glorious, beautiful, infinitely sexy . . .' he said the words slowly, tasting them on his tongue, taking fistfuls of the softness and winding it loosely around his hands, drawing her mouth back to his. Her arms went around his waist under the jacket, locking him closer.

His hands stroked her hair and it clung, crackling, to him like a live thing. Sarah's mind blurred and tumbled weightlessly, the song of the crickets outside merging to vibrate with the high, unending song of longing that Max was creating with his hands and mouth. Like a virtuoso with a beloved instrument, he handled her with consummate skill, touching the chords of forgotten notes, discovering new ones.

At some point her dress slithered into an insubstantial

heap at their feet and Sarah shivered at the friction of his clothes on her heated skin.

'Still no compliments for me, darling vixen?' Max taunted softly, forcing her back over his arm so that the weight of her hair pulled her head back, but she could only moan helplessly, eyelids fluttering closed not wanting him to stop. Not wanting him to ever stop . . .

'It seems I shall have to use force . . .' and he took the bare sacrifice of her throat, trailing fire with his lips and tongue to the taut offering of her breasts. Tiny cries escaped her as he kissed the captured peaks, his mouth opening, moist, knowing, as he explored her arousal with a sensual expertise that had her twisting in voluptuous agony.

'Give in?' as his mouth returned to hers for the final onslaught.

'Yes . . . yes . . . yes to everything . . . please . . .' Sarah felt disorientated and clutched wildly at him as she felt herself whirling, falling, but he was only pushing her down to the soft white sheepskin rug beneath their feet.

It seemed an age that he stood staring at her as she lay, satin body framed in auburn silk, a strip of delicate black lace her only covering. Then slowly, deliberately, Max stripped off his jacket and tie and threw them down, tugging open his shirt, scattering cufflinks with a soft patter across the floor, and then threw the discarded shirt down, too.

The smooth olive skin gleamed bronze in the lamplight, silvered with dampness and rippling as he moved to kneel beside her. He plunged his hands into the broad swathes of her hair and lifted them, letting the strands run through his fingers like water to splash over her body.

'How could I ever have thought you anything but what you are—lovely, desirable . . .' His voice roughened into harshness and his hands clenched her waist. 'My God, I want you—'

Breathless with impatience Sarah reached up to pull

him down, flesh against flesh, stroking her hands over his chest and shoulders, feeling him shudder like a man with a fever at her eager touch. He shifted his weight over her and her fingers flexed, nails sinking into his back as she felt the powerful thrust of his body.

'Don't hurt me, sweet vixen, I'm at your mercy now,' he groaned as her nails raked downwards but she was beyond controlling herself, her body arched like a bow to his, her head rolling helplessly from side to side in an erotic transport of delight, all consciousness lost to the foaming excitement as the waves of sweet, piercing pleasure built up to tidal force. There were a thousand exquisite pulse-beats in her body; resounding desire in every cell and nerve ending.

The frantic movements of her body beneath his took the final shreds of his own control. There were no concessions now to her doubts, but she welcomed him, mind and body longing for the release that he had been so skilfully denying them both, hands seeking the belt buckle that dug into the soft flesh of her belly.

The interruption, when it came, came with brutal suddenness. A splash, a curse, a muffled thud and an explosion of bright white light from the direction of the half-closed bedroom door.

Max was on his feet even before Sarah's sluggish brain registered what had happened. She lay for a moment, dazed, shaking, gulping great breaths of air, then jack-knifed up to grab the flimsy dress that lay an arm's length away. She stared blearily at the door with an awful premonition of disaster.

'Is that you, love? It's only me. I know I said I'd be away for a day or two—' Roy broke off, aghast, as he appeared in the doorway and saw the two frozen figures.

'Roy!' Sarah despaired and the unexplainable guilt she felt must have shown on her face for Max looked from the other man to her with dawning suspicion. Roy was wrapped only in a towel and dripped damply on to the floorboards. We're all undressed, thought Sarah with hysterical irrelevancy ... with Max, of course, wearing the most of all!'

He stooped now, to shrug into his shirt, and to pick up his jacket and tie, which he thrust into the pocket.

'My mistake,' he said with bleak and deadly quietness and Sarah recoiled at the brief look of icy hostility he gave her as he passed by. Her throat was so jammed full of anger and explanation that she choked helplessly, unable to utter a word.

Max hesitated at the top of the stairwell, half-turned towards Roy and, unbelievingly, Sarah heard her friend repeat with contemptuous precision:

'Your mistake.'

Sarah squeezed her eyes shut on the nightmare, but the distant, distinct click of the front door confirmed the sick reality.

'Wait here,' she heard Roy say as he ducked back into the bathroom. Where did he think she would go? Dashing out half naked into the street after Max? The thought prompted her to scramble up and pull on her dress, doing up the zip with clumsy fingers. Her whole body was racked with agonising cramps, she felt as though part of her had been torn away, leaving a great, gaping wound.

'What was he doing here?' Roy came back into the room wearing denim jeans and carrying a white T-shirt screwed into a ball. She could hear bathwater gurgling down the pipes.

'What do you think he was doing?' She found her voice, small and tight. 'I would have thought it was pretty obvious. What were *you* doing? You aren't even supposed to be in Auckland!'

Roy shrugged, unembarrassed. 'My car broke down on the motorway, so I called the trip off until it's fixed. I didn't get back until late and I was filthy, I needed a bath.'

'At—' Sarah looked at her watch and gasped. 'At midnight!' She and Max had been here for nearly an hour. The pain and frustration intensified.

Roy ran his hand through his wet hair. 'Is it that late? I

came over about ten—you weren't here so I let myself in
. . . I thought I'd just have a quick dip. I must have fallen
asleep. Where were you?'

'Dinner. We went to dinner. You shouldn't have come
in, Roy,' her voice rose sharply.

'All right, I'm sorry, there's no need to shout,' he said.
'You've never come back with anyone before, how did I
know tonight was going to be different? I've used your
bath before at night, and I didn't fall asleep on purpose,
just to break up your cute little scene with the boss.'

Furiously angry, Sarah lashed out with her tongue. She
had never until now regretted the closeness of their
friendship and in the short, heated exchange that followed
said hurtful things that were unfair and untrue, and was
stung in turn by Roy's retaliations.

'And who the hell are you to make sarcastic remarks
about cute scenes! You're the one who told me I was only
half a woman,' Sarah finished desperately.

'I didn't mean you to jump into bed with the first man
who asked you. I thought you had more self-respect.'

Sarah stiffened. 'You make it sound cheap and
sordid—'

'Instead of romantic? Come off it, Sarah, you're not the
type for one-night stands with strangers.'

'He is not a stranger and it wasn't a one-night stand,'
said Sarah icily. Instinctively she knew that the passion
she and Max had shared was more than just a brief,
animal urge easily satiated.

'If you were capable of going to bed with a man without
any kind of emotional involvement you would have done
so by now, taken the easy solace it offered,' Roy continued
implacably. 'I may be an advocate of free love, but not free
sex. There has to be a relationship first!'

'But there was!' Why did he find that so hard to accept?
'You don't understand—' and to her shame and horror
Sarah burst into a flood of tears.

Instantly she found herself enfolded in a great bear-
hug, her head pressed against Roy's damp chest.

'Don't cry, honey,' he rocked her. 'You never cry. I'm sorry, I don't know what came over me. I was just shocked, I guess, I let rip without thinking. You must be feeling ghastly. I'm sorry.' The words rumbled reassuringly in the ear that was pressed against his chest. Roy was Roy again, and not that accusing stranger.

She let herself be led over to the two-seater settee against the wall and felt herself pushed into the squashy cushions. She sat, sniffing, feeling drained and deathly tired.

'I'm the one who should be saying sorry,' she said at last, wiping her face on the offered T-shirt and handing it back to the hunched figure beside her. 'I yelled first. I didn't mean what I said. I don't know what came over *me*.'

'I do.'

She coloured. 'Oh God, what must he be thinking!'

'Nothing complimentary,' he replied in an odd, flat voice.

'I should have said something . . . but I couldn't. I couldn't believe it was happening.' She turned. 'But you said something. Why did you say that? It implied—'

Roy pulled moodily at his beard, avoiding her eyes. 'What should I have said—"we're just good friends"?'

'You could have said—'

'Look, Sarah, he was in no mood to listen to anything —reasonable or unreasonable.'

She remembered the glacial look and winced. No. Max had drawn his own conclusions. He thought he had been made a fool of, used as a stop-gap while her live-in lover was away. But, remembering also what they had shared, she did not think that he would believe that for long. Once he had had time to consider he would realise that there must be another explanation. They would probably even be able to share a rueful laugh over the incident. Should she ring him? No, better wait until tomorrow and speak to him face to face. He would probably hang up on her in his present mood. And she had better ponder on the best approach to take.

When Roy saw some of the tension leaving her face, he chanced a gentle probe.

'What sparked this sudden mutual interest then?'

'Not sudden,' Sarah yawned, the late hour catching up with her.

'Regular date, huh?' he jeered lightly.

'Regular from now on,' she grinned.

Roy slumped back on the settee, frowning. 'I never thought you would be attracted to a man like that,' he muttered. 'I thought you had more taste.'

Fleetingly, Sarah wondered at his tone. Could he be jealous? Then she dismissed the thought as ridiculous. Roy might love her, but only in a brotherly way.

'A man like what?' she asked.

'A cunning, cold-blooded, worthless bastard,' Roy said in a grim, alien voice.

'Roy!' Sarah sat up, utterly confounded. 'How can you say that? You don't even know the man.'

'I know enough. Next time I see that lecherous swine I'll punch his head in!'

'Roy!' There was no doubting his sincerity. 'He didn't rape me! He was here because I wanted him to be. Are you going to do this every time I bring home a man you don't approve of?'

He gave a twisted grin. 'You sound as if you're planning to bring them home by the dozen. No. Just this one. He's special.'

'That's why he was here,' Sarah told him. 'Actually, when he first asked me to have dinner with him, yesterday on the island, I wasn't sure either. But—'

'Yesterday?' Roy's flaming head snapped round.

'Yes. During the cruise.'

'He asked you out? Yesterday?' It was unlike Roy to be so slow on the uptake.

'Not until after we'd kissed,' said Sarah impishly, but Roy didn't smile, he looked quite white and taking pity on him Sarah told him all about her meeting with Max and their subsequent roller-coaster relationship. If anything,

Roy began to look sicker, so she threw in the story about *Images*.

'Why the hell didn't you tell me all this?' he demanded hoarsely. 'You hardly ever mentioned him. I had no idea you had such close contacts with the guy!'

'I didn't want to talk about him,' said Sarah, aware of how lame that sounded. 'I didn't even think I *liked* him.'

'Oh God!' Roy buried his face in his hands.

'What's the matter?'

'You're not going to like this.' He lifted his head apologetically.

'Is it something you've heard about him? I probably know it already,' said Sarah confidently.

'Why do you think he immediately assumed that we were lovers, not just living together—or brother and sister, or cousins or something?'

'I told him I had no family here . . . and that I lived alone.' One way and another she had told him quite a bit about herself in the course of the evening.

'He and I have met before, Sarah.'

'You never told me,' she said, surprised.

'You never told me about you and him,' Roy pointed out. 'Anyway we only met this morning. At Carerra's gallery. He was opening the exhibition.'

A starburst exploded in Sarah's brain. Max's strange mood, his intense curiosity, the way he had looked at her and talked—the look on his face when she had let down her hair.

'You showed him the painting,' she breathed, appalled. 'You let him see it!' Her voice peaked on a squeak.

'No . . . at least—' Roy spread spatulate hands help-lessly. 'It was Carerra. When I said it was for sale overseas he dashed off and came back with Wilde in tow.'

Sarah groaned.

'I didn't know who he was,' protested Roy. 'Carerra was fluttering around like a mother hen, and when he got around to introducing us it was too late. I had no idea there was anything between you and Wilde—especially since I could have sworn he didn't recognise you. Why should he? The resemblance is quite slight to the casual eye.'

'His eye is never casual,' stressed Sarah.

'Well, he didn't say anything . . . although he did ask later who the model was.'

'Oh God—'

'But only in a casual way when we were discussing some technical points. I said you were a friend.'

'A friend,' echoed Sarah stupidly. No wonder Max had jumped to the wrong conclusion. That beautiful, damning painting. It gave her a strange, curling sensation in her stomach to think of him standing there before that canvas, studying her naked image. Somehow it seemed more indecent than when he had done so in the flesh.

'He didn't comment. Perhaps he didn't know it was you,' said Roy without hope.

'He knew all right.' Her skin tingled when she remembered the fire in Max's eyes when he saw her hair swirl down around her hips. 'But why didn't he say anything at dinner?'

'He would have to be insensitive not to realise why the painting wasn't being offered for public sale here. He was probably waiting for you to tell him.'

'It never even occurred to me,' said Sarah absently. He *had* given her several openings, she realised now, but she had ignored them. Such mundane matters had been far from her mind! 'What did he say about it?' she asked, stricken with curiosity.

' "Exceptionally fine",' Roy gave a creditable imitation of Max's drawl and grinned. 'Among other things. I rather liked him. Knows his art, has a shrewd intelligence, and wasn't the least impressed by Carerra's outrageous flattery.'

'So how come you were uptight about me coming back here with such an admirable character?'

He winced at her sarcasm. 'Brainstorm, darlin'; still half asleep, etc. As good at jumping to conclusions as he is.

I thought I'd read him all wrong, that he was one of those slimy creeps whose interest in art is covertly prurient. I thought he was getting his kicks from possessing the original of a work of art, so to speak.'

'You thought an awful lot in a very short time.'

'Didn't I just. And way off beam, too.'

'Were you?' She *wanted* to think so, but wanting didn't make something so.

Roy seemed to understand what was in her mind. '*I* think so. If he was as corrupt as all that he would have left with a wave and a philosophical shrug. Instead he looked like a man who had just received a massive kick in the guts—'

'As poetical as ever,' said Sarah to hide her relief. Roy could be trusted to read facial expressions, he had made his fame and fortune from them.

'Anyway, his interest in you obviously started way back. He spotted your potential and had the means and desire to exploit it. I'm not surprised that his desires took a more personal turn, they often do between model and artist—witness you and Simon, and me and—' he ticked a few names off his fingers and Sarah laughed. 'I won't say that seeing the painting mightn't have spiced the dish for him; it's not a clinical study after all, but the main ingredient is you. On brief analysis, I'd say he was too cultured to equate art with pornography and too virile to need the stimulation that pornography provides, hmmm?' Green eyes crinkled as Sarah began to fiddle intently with her hair, twisting it into a long tail, and he continued musingly, 'In fact, he would make a good subject. I'd like to resolve some of those complexities on canvas.'

'Perhaps you could do a nude,' Sarah needled.

'Sorry,' he gathered himself. 'Just thinking aloud. Though he certainly has the body for it.'

'Goodnight, Roy.' The sly dig shot Sarah to her feet.

'Okay, okay, I'm going, I can take a hint. Will you be all right?'

'I'm not about to commit suicide,' Sarah said in revenge. 'Not over a cold-blooded, worthless—'

'Don't repeat that, will you? It was quite an excusable error.'

'In quite a comedy of errors.' Sarah walked over to the balcony door and slid it open.

'Never mind, all's well that ends well,' Roy punned. 'If you need a written statement to convince your once and future lover of our platonic friendship, just ask.' Sarah pushed him out the door, but he poked his head back in to add:

'I hope you don't singe your wings with this one, love. He's a high-flyer.'

Sarah sighed as she shut the door after him. She was touched by his concern but he was worrying unnecessarily. She wasn't going to make the mistake of taking Max's attentions seriously. They were worlds apart. But who knew better than she that vows of permanency held no guarantees of permanent happiness? A temporary adult relationship, brief, satisfying, compromising no one, suited them both.

She turned off the light and padded across the floor to the bedroom, wincing as she trod on something hard. She felt around in the darkness and picked up the forgotten cufflinks. Here was a ready-made excuse to speak to Max tomorrow. There would be a few nasty minutes to brave but it would be worth it. He was worldly, sophisticated, had a well-developed sense of humour—he had displayed some of it tonight. He would understand, once she explained. She fell into bed, warmed by the certainty and slept, deep and dreamless.

CHAPTER TEN

SWATHED in protective towels, Sarah stared at her reflection in the large mirror rimmed with lights.

Teresa had surpassed herself this time. Her swan-song, she called it, for later this afternoon she was flying on to another assignment in Australia. Sarah's hair had been swept up into a soft, romantic knot secured by red enamel combs and trailing short, feathered wisps at the sides and nape of her neck. Her face had been subtly rounded out with blusher and highlighter and a dramatic blend of silver-grey, blue and violet on her eyelids and a provocative deep red gloss on her lips drew attention away from the pointed jawline to the central features.

It was a sophisticated, elaborate mask and the white walls in the background and white towels around her neck gave her head a floating, disembodied look.

Sarah shivered, not at the macabre thought but on recalling her brief encounter with Max that morning. She had arrived at work full of determination, relieved to find Max alone in the office, poring over a series of marketing surveys. It encouraged her to see that he looked so normal, no clouds of thunder lowered upon his head.

'Can I see you?' she had asked, after greeting him, standing tentatively in front of his desk.

'You see me now.' He read on. Not so encouraging. Still, who would expect him to be effusive after the night's fiasco?

'I . . .' she fumbled in her bag. 'I want to return these . . .' she placed the cufflinks on the desk and stared hard at the dark crown of his head, willing it to lift.

'Thank you.' He wrote something in the margin on one of the sheets, and added a footnote.

'And . . . I want to explain; about last night,' she said mesmerised by the pen flowing smoothly over the paper.

'I wasn't aware that the situation required clarification,' came the tinder-dry comment.

'But it does.' *Look at me, damn you*, she longed to say, as he had said to her. But of course she didn't. She kept her voice quiet and steady.

'I know it must have looked . . . well, odd. But—Roy is the friend I mentioned. We don't live together; he lives next door—'

'How convenient,' he said pleasantly. His pen paused and he looked at her for the first time since she had entered the room. The hazel eyes had a strange, opaque quality, quite empty of expression.

Ignoring her sinking heart Sarah rushed untidily into her story, about Roy and the trip, and the hot water cylinder, and his habit of falling asleep in the bath. Shorn of background and atmosphere it sounded painfully thin, even to Sarah. The more she became aware of it the more tangled her explanation became. He listened with an impassive, unblinking, lack of interest for a few minutes before cutting in as she faltered for a third time:

'What are you so uptight about? Forget it, Sarah, it doesn't matter.' He smiled, a thin unpleasant smile that went no further than a faint movement of the lips. 'Post-mortems bore me.'

He bent his head again, adding, a few seconds later when he became aware that she was still standing there, stunned:

'Teresa's waiting for you in the studio. Let's get this over and done with, shall we?'

Nobody, but nobody, ignored Max when he spoke in that clipped, impatient fashion, not even Sarah at her bravest, and at that moment her bravery was at its lowest ebb. His studied indifference had a devastating effect on her self-confidence. Did he really care so little? Or was it all a front? With Max it was difficult to tell.

Sarah stretched out a hand to touch the dress which

hung alongside the mirror. Perhaps he wouldn't be so indifferent when he saw her in that. He had been mildly complimentary at the fitting and mild approval from Max was equivalent of rave reviews from anyone else. Perhaps he needed something to jolt him into remembrance of what they had shared, of the husky words of promise he had murmured to her last night. This dress could do it, if anything could. It was beautiful.

The long, pure silk dress was the same toffee-apple-red colour as her lips, the broad straps supporting a low, square-cut bodice, the narrow waist stitched in a V-shape at the front, giving the dress a slightly medieval look, with the skirt falling in soft folds to the floor. Over the bodice fitted a high-necked, long-sleeved silk chiffon camisole, embroidered with dark red sequins, fluttering to a scarfed hem at waist-level.

'Sorry to be so long,' Teresa bounced through the door carrying a pair of strappy red high-heeled shoes which she stood neatly under the hanging dress. 'I must learn to organise myself more . . . Now, where was I? A dab of freshener to set you, I think. Are they ready yet, do you know?'

'Mike's still setting up.' Sarah closed her eyes as the other girl dabbed on some cold, fragrant lotion with a cotton wool ball. Then with a flick of her wrist she whipped off Sarah's cloak of towels, eyeing the two wisps of lace which were all she wore underneath.

'I know you complain about skinniness being the fashion, but I wouldn't mind a few of your curves. It's almost a pity to put on the dress. If you walked around like that you wouldn't have to worry about make-up. No one would look at you above the neck!'

'This is supposed to be an Autumn Collection,' Sarah grinned, used to Teresa's frankness by now.

'That's better. You looked a bit down in the mouth—' she broke off as the door swung open behind them. Sarah's whole body tensed as she saw the reflection of their visitor.

'You could have knocked,' Teresa said, in her mildly bossy tone.

'Sarah's not shy. Are you, Sarah?' Her heartbeat accelerated as she briefly met sardonic eyes in the mirror. Was he going to say something in front of Teresa? She looked hastily around for her towels, but they had already been stuffed into the laundry bag in the far corner of the room and not for anything was Sarah going to stand up and expose herself to that subjective appraisal.

'That's not the point,' said Teresa, unaware of the undercurrents. 'It can be most off-putting to have people barging in on you unexpectedly.'

Fortunately, Max wasn't required to make a reply for at that moment Julie poked her head around the half-open door.

'Excuse me, Max. I know you're not set up yet, can I borrow Teresa for a few minutes? I need some advice and I might not get the chance to ask her later on.'

'Ten minutes,' said Max, not taking his eyes off Sarah.

'Thanks.' She disappeared and Teresa took off her thin protective wrap and hung it on the hook on the back of the door.

'Don't do anything I wouldn't do,' she said cheekily, as she scampered out after Julie.

The skin prickled all the way down Sarah's bare spine but she controlled the impulse to squirm. He had taken off the light jacket he had worn in the office, she noted as her eyes avoided his, to reveal a cool white shirt, tailored in some rough linen weave, tucked into oatmeal trousers with a snakeskin belt. He had rolled up his sleeves for work in the hot studio and undone two shirt buttons, and the black mist of body hair on his forearms and rising from his chest brought back memories that made Sarah swallow nervously. She cleared her throat. By now she should be used to the way that Max used silence as an intimidating weapon.

'Would you mind passing me that wrap behind you?'

'A bit late to worry about covering yourself up, isn't it?' he said laconically.

'It's quite cool in here,' Sarah said with incredible casualness.

'Odd. Such a small room. And no air-conditioning.'

There wasn't either, Sarah suddenly noticed, and flushed furiously, glaring at him. He was using that sarcastic, supercilious voice she so detested. The more so because she suspected it was assumed. He wasn't looking in the least bored.

'And I don't like being stared at,' she said rashly.

'You surprise me.' Icicles dripped from every syllable.

'I thought that was what interested you .. my unexpectedness,' she mocked softly and for a moment the bored mask slipped and hazel eyes blazed yellowly at her, to be veiled immediately. But Sarah felt a surge of triumph. She had penetrated that blank façade, now she must cut off his retreat. Get his anger out in the open where she could fight it. She twisted round in the chair to look at him properly. He was a long way up. 'Do you think that I'm an exhibitionist simply because I have my picture painted?' She caught the thought which hardened his face. 'All right, it was in the nude but Roy is a fine artist, a serious and dedicated man. I wouldn't have posed otherwise.'

His eyes had flickered at the mention of Roy. 'Oh, I agree he's good. It's a superb piece of work. So good that one can forgive it its sheer dishonesty.'

'Dishonesty!' She felt a prick of anger on Roy's behalf. 'That's unfair. Roy has great integrity, he's the most decent and honest man I know!'

'Then I pity him!' Sarah shrank from the full force of his contempt, shocked by its intensity, beginning to appreciate the magnitude of the task she had set herself. He turned and she thought, with a mixture of fear and relief, that he was going to walk out. But, ominously, he merely closed the door, then leaned his long length against it while his narrowed eyes crawled slowly over her half-naked body. 'Does he still see you as the innocent temptress? I doubt it, after last night. No one's that gullible.'

'Will you pass me the wrap, please?' Sarah asked, waveringly.

'You're not showing me anything I haven't already seen.' Carelessly he unhooked the wrap and tossed it across, watching cynically as she put it on and stood up to tighten the belt, facing him proudly. 'Less, thanks to your . . . shall we say, enthusiasm? And your . . . *friend's* artistic skill. Next time, though, he should paint you as you are. A temptress indeed, but with all the innocence of a whore!'

'I thought post-mortems bored you,' Sarah said, stunned by his crudity but still grimly holding on to her composure.

'I thought that would hit home,' he told her, betraying pleasure. 'Incredible, isn't it, that any man could resist your injured innocent act?'

'I hope you enjoyed your petty revenge,' Sarah threw at him fiercely. 'So much for your much-vaunted sense of justice! You won't listen to the facts because you don't want to hear anything that will challenge your infallible assumptions!'

'The operative word being facts, not your brand of pretty fiction,' he said with bitter clarity. 'There's nothing wrong with a whore, as long as she's an honest whore.'

'You have a twisted sense of morality,' Sarah choked in wrathful indignation. 'No wonder you confuse fact and fiction. You were taking me to bed last night, not to church, and it's only your pride and vanity that got hurt. You're not going to save face by indulging in cheap name-calling—'

Max elbowed himself off the door with a suddenness that had Sarah clutching the chair between them.

'Cheap?' he snarled. 'Why not? You were mine for the price of a meal!'

'And you were mine for nothing,' Sarah flung back. 'What does that make you?'

His nostrils thinned. 'At least I offer exclusivity.'

Sarah laughed; a shrill, brittle sound. 'Of what? Club membership? Mistresses and ex-mistresses of Max Wilde? I thought *that* was open to the public.'

'Jealous?' he thrust, harshly mocking, and something inside Sarah writhed briefly and died.

'Of you? Don't be ridiculous!' she spat, tempted to throw the chair full in his sneering face. 'I was just pointing out that you're the last one to preach morals to me. Maybe you're too corrupt to be able to understand that a man and woman can have a platonic relationship like Roy and I. Well, I don't give a damn what you think anymore. Roy and I have known each other for seven years. He was a good friend of Simon's, and of mine—'

'I'll bet he was,' Max inserted silkily. 'And with whom was he the more intimate—your husband . . . or you?'

'You . . . vile . . . hypocritical *swine*,' Sarah gasped out, flushed and trembling so hard she had to grip the back of the chair. Leaning into it frantically, eyes glittering brilliantly, she was unaware of how excited and exciting she looked in the grip of raging temper. 'How dare you make such foul, such *rotten* accusations. You know *nothing*. You're a bigot and a coward—you're *afraid* to listen, to admit any weakness or wrong, because that would mean you'd have to come down off your self-created Olympus and let the rest of us see how fallible, how *human* you are! You're not a god, Max—I don't think you know what you are!'

The narrow face darkened and Max made an indistinct sound in his throat, hands curling slowly into fists at his sides, balls of bone and muscle. He took a step towards her, as if he couldn't help himself and Sarah recoiled, letting the chair fall with a sharp clatter. He wouldn't resort to physical violence would he?

'It won't work, Sarah, not this time,' he told her through his teeth. 'I know you now for what you are: a treacherous, amoral little slut!' His mouth twisted in contempt, his voice filled with loathing. 'You're clever, I'll give you that—a woman has to be to fool me. But I never make the same mistake twice.' He took on a cruel mimicry: '*I don't remember ever feeling like this*. You must have a singularly short memory!'

Each word was a drop of acid etching itself into her fiery brain. Sarah tugged the thin wrap tighter, as if it could protect her from the merciless onslaught. The whole situation had exploded in her face and she was too hurt now to retract anything, or even want to. Perhaps she had provoked him, but only because she refused to be ground into the dirt as a result of his intransigence.

As she hugged herself, drawing the slippery material taut over her breasts, she saw the smouldering eyes drop by the merest flicker of a lash and fix themselves again on her face with a strained intensity. And suddenly it hit her *why* he was so bitterly contemptuous and how she could exact bitter payment for all his insults.

She rubbed her crossed hands up and down her arms, feigning weariness, watching Max's reaction through lowered lashes, noting the way his eyes unwillingly followed the slow, massaging movements. *Yes*. She let one hand drop and moved the other casually up to slide inside the neckline of the wrap. A muscle jumped in the lean jaw as she shifted the material slightly so that he had a brief glimpse of golden bare skin to her waist, the more enticing because it was now supposedly concealed.

'What's the matter, Max?' she asked huskily. 'Does my body bother you?' His eyes jerked back to her face, shocked, and she gave him a slow smile. 'Not bored, Max. Never bored. My body fascinates you, doesn't it . . . my body, my hair. Did you dream about it last night? What you missed, what you wanted . . .'

Dark blood ran up under the taut skin of his face and Sarah felt a hot, hard thump of victory in her chest. 'Poor Max,' she simpered. 'I turned you on and you don't know how to turn yourself off . . .'

He cracked wide open then, in a way that appalled her even as it sent adrenalin racing through her veins. The hard, arrogant lines of his face blurred with rage, the eyes insensate and she panicked immediately, realising that in driving him over the edge she too had lost what little control she had.

He came towards her, off the balls of his feet, and she held up a feeble hand to ward him off.

'No, Max—I didn't mean—'

'Oh yes, you did, you—' he struck her hand away, backing her up to one smooth, blank white wall. 'Haven't you got the guts to finish what you started?'

'No—' she whispered, terrified at the demon she had released; at her own swirling, reckless excitement.

'Are you a masochist as well as a nymphomaniac? On the lookout for new sensations. By God, I'll give you one!'

He reached for her, and reacting instinctively Sarah clawed at him with elegant blood-red nails, but he shackled her wrists with steely fingers, holding her at bay. 'Hit me, Sarah, and I'll hit you back. The only reason I didn't last time was because I thought you were a lady. But the lady's a tramp.' A thin razor-sharp smile sliced into her. 'You're the hypocrite, not me. I never pretended to be inexperienced, and at least I'm capable of being faithful to one woman at a time. My lovers don't have to worry about queues in the bathroom.'

'I didn't know he was there,' she moaned, stupidly, hardly aware of what she was saying. He was just talking to feed the inferno inside him, building up to an explosive climax. His face, so close to hers, looked gaunt, scraped to the bone.

'No? Maybe threesomes turn you on. Was I supposed to ask him to join us?'

'You're disgusting.' She turned her burning cheek aside, but he was relentless, remorseless.

'He looked fairly shattered, though. Did he kick you out after I left? But no doubt you've kept other options open . . . was I going to be one of them?'

'Bastard,' she gritted, closing her eyes against the withering scorn, feeling the hot salty pressure against her lids.

'A whore and a bastard. Perhaps we're made for each other. Shall we find out?'

Slowly, inexorably, he pulled her wrists up and out until her arms were spreadeagled along the wall. She fought him every inch of the way, silently, with all her strength, but her futile struggles seemed to compound his enjoyment.

'You're getting excited, darling,' he drawled savagely into her hectic face. 'Does it excite you to be handled roughly? Is that all part of the game?'

He moved on to her, anchoring the centre of her body to the wall with his hips, his every deliberate action exuding sexual menace that was frightening and repelling. Yet dark, furious, threatening, he was still attractive and Sarah moved frantically, trying to twist away, horribly aware of something inside her that was responding to the physical stimulus. He laughed and laid the full length of his body against hers, rock-hard muscle from shoulder to knee and she was shaken by a compulsive, betraying shiver.

'No, please . . . not like this,' she cried weakly and the answer came, raw and insolent:

'Hell, isn't it, Sarah, when you want something you know you shouldn't? Beg if you must, but try and make it a little more convincing!'

He lowered his mouth to hers, taking his time, indicating he would use all his considerable skill to get what he wanted—complete submission. When she kept her mouth obstinately closed he moved sharply, crushing her against the wall until the pain in her shoulder-blades made her give a muffled sob. Immediately the enemy invaded the vulnerable territory, thrusting a coaxing, questing tongue into the deep moistness, tasting victory. Whichever way she moved her head he followed easily and soon she stopped, feeling hot and helpless and giddy, accepting him. He began to grind his hips against hers in a slow, sensual rhythm that mimicked the act of possession, rousing a sweet, familiar ache that made a mockery of

Sarah's protest. But acquiescence wasn't enough for him and he kept up the forcible arousal until stark, awful reality faded and Sarah was swept back into a world of pure sensation, of touch and taste and feel. An involuntary groan broke from her lips as the blood began to throb at her pulse points, sing along her veins.

The sound was absorbed into his mouth as he loosened his hold on her wrists, keeping her pinned with his body while he untied the belt at her waist.

She freed her mouth long enough to plead:

'No, Max—someone might come . . .'

'Let them.'

He kissed her again, and again, overcoming her brief resistance, roughly stripping the wrap from her shoulders, baring her body to his touch. His mouth was warm on her neck and she felt his practised hands run knowingly over her tingling skin, her body lifting and tautening to meet them. Desire raced along sensitive nerve endings and she moaned softly as his fingers stroked down the silken curve of her breast, slipping inside her flimsy bra to find and caress the burgeoning nipple.

Her trembling increased. She was made for this, this blissful pleasure; and he to reveal it to her. It felt good. It felt right.

She whispered his name, hands coming up to settle on the soft dark hair at his nape, cupping the shape of his head.

It seemed to trigger a nerve and suddenly she felt him shudder and tense, swearing thickly against her throat, a vicious sound of self-disgust that tore the lovely fabric of her dream. He thrust himself violently away from her and she swayed, mind blunted by sensation, skin incandescent with heat, damp palms pressing back against the cool of the wall behind her.

With an effort Sarah lifted heavy lids, bewildered at the swiftness of his withdrawal. Max had his back to her, bending stiffly to pick up the fallen chair and straighten it meticulously. His shirt was clinging damply to his skin and she saw the muscles beneath clench briefly before he turned around.

'Well, that's one thing you don't have to lie about. You certainly seem to get job satisfaction.' He wiped the redness from his mouth with the back of his hand as though the taste of her revolted him.

Sarah steadied herself against the wall, the only stable thing in a shifting universe. She sought his face for some indication of passion, of softness, but there was none. Savage lines of satisfaction grained the skin around his mouth and his eyes were like knives, cold and merciless, dissecting her.

Her stomach lurched violently. She felt bruised, violated. What had happened to her self-respect? He had treated her with the same contempt that a rapist must feel for his victim; with anger and disgust. And she had enjoyed it! Invited it even, for she had provoked him to breaking point. God, what was the matter with her? She was acting as if every vile thing he said about her was true!

She watched, hypnotised as he tore a tissue out of the large box on the make-up table and wiped his mouth and hand. Then he began to sort through the lipsticks until he matched one with the smear on the tissue.

'No!' Her skin crawled as she realised what he intended to do.

He smiled cruelly. 'Lost your taste for being touched? If you prefer, you can wait for Teresa . . . explain to her how you smudged her good works.'

Sarah submitted frozenly as he tilted her chin to the light and skilfully re-coloured her bloodless lips. She could see the faint beading of sweat on his upper lip, but his hand performed its task without a tremor. He was inhuman. How could he do it . . . while she stood there beaten, humiliated . . . she remembered her wrap and scrabbled blindly for the gaping edges.

'Thanks for letting me test the merchandise.' He threw the lipstick back on to the table. 'But I think you've overestimated its value. You ought to consider the strategic advantages of withholding your assets.'

Sarah didn't have the strength to fight back, she leaned her head tiredly against the wall and stayed unmoving until she heard him leave.

She collapsed at last on to the chair, blinking fiercely. It would take ages to repair the damage if she cried, and *he* would know the reason for the delay. She would not give him such a complete triumph.

She hated him. He was arrogant and crude and so *wrong*. She wasn't promiscuous . . . she didn't think . . . at least, only with him. But why? Was it only because he had been the first to tap the deep well of her suppressed sexuality? She could see, from the bleak vantage point of a new physical maturity, that Simon had never done more than skim the surface of her passions. He had been too selfishly concerned with his own needs to be able to fully satisfy hers. Max, on the other hand, confident of his prowess, had been willing to wait on her, taking as much pleasure in discovering what pleased her as in fulfilling his own desires . . . in fact they had seemed inseparable.

Sarah buried her face in her hands and groaned. Her hands felt icy, her body numb. That was twice in two days Max had brought her to the pitch of desire then abandoned her, though this second time was by far the worst. She shouldn't have tried to fight him, he could always annihilate her physically and verbally. She couldn't even feel angry at him, though she had every reason to be . . . just this terrible numbness.

It was pride alone that saw her through the nightmare session that followed. Pride made her smile, and sparkle and *project* by order of the shadowy figure beyond the half-circle of bright lights, when inside she felt shrivelled and old.

Afterwards, in the semblance of normality, she allowed herself to be bullied into going to lunch with Tom, though the thought of food was nauseating. They went to a tiny coffee bar not far from the office, one they had been to several times before, situated below street level, down a narrow flight of stairs.

Playing with her salad Sarah let Tom's ramblings about the new contract with *Rags*' printer, the busy London schedule he would be returning to at the end of the week, and other inconsequentials flow soothingly around her. Suddenly, out of the blue, he said something that riveted her attention.

'Max came under duress? What kind of duress?' It was no use telling herself she wasn't interested.

'He only agreed to come out to New Zealand in exchange for certain . . . ah . . . concessions in the boardroom,' Tom explained, seemingly absorbed in the disposition of tea-leaves in the bottom of his cup. 'Sir Richard insisted that he take a break from his rigorous routine, but Max would have none of that, so *Rags & Riches* was a compromise on both sides.' Tom paused maddeningly. He was being uncharacteristically indiscreet and Sarah prayed he wasn't going to realise it now and clam up. If she had been thinking more clearly she might have wondered about his sudden desire to impart gratuitous information on a hitherto avoided subject.

'Max resigned himself, if only because he knew it was basically his own fault. When he came out of hospital after his accident he was ordered to convalesce for at least a month. Instead he put himself under psychological pressure to perform, and at a level which exceeded even his pre-accident optimum.'

He lost interest in reading tea-leaves and watched Sarah as she grappled with the one fact that she had plucked out of his statement. *He* had told her—but she hadn't believed—those scars hadn't looked so awful . . .

'Accident?' came out shrill and cracked.

Blue, blue eyes, calm and unfathomable as the sea, looked into hers. 'It was played down at the time: these things can and do upset the balance of the market. Last April Max crashed his plane on a flight from Paris to London. Nearly killed himself—'

Somebody was operating a drill in her head. The bright red-flocked wallpaper of the coffee bar sprang at her, sharp, vivid, threatening suffocation, and the warm, spicy coffee-laden air grew strong and bitter in her nostrils, a sour bitterness that also flooded the back of her throat.

'I'm sorry, love, but at least it was quick. They said he would have been killed on impact . . .' Roy's caring voice floated through her chaotic mind. Killed? Had Max been killed? Her whole body was one silent, suffering, scream.

No. *Nearly.* That's what Tom had said. Nearly. A year ago she hadn't even been aware of Max's existence, let alone . . . The world began to revolve slowly around her, then faster, and cold sweat broke out on her forehead as she groped for meaning. She laid her head in her arms on the table, waiting for the turbulence to subside, hoping she wasn't going to disgrace herself by being sick. If he had died, she would never have met him. Never have fought those exhilarating battles; and won, and lost, and hated, and loved. *And loved.*

The numbness of the past hour dissolved as a wave of terrible futility washed over her, flooding her with exquisite pain. She loved him! That was why she lit up like a torch whenever he touched her, that was why his indifference, his rejection had been so utterly devastating. She loved him. In spite of herself, in spite of him . . . the man who never used the word *love*, except in the physical sense. God, it was almost funny!

'Sarah, are you all right?' A voice penetrated the fog.

She lifted her head. 'Yes. Yes. I just felt a bit odd there for a moment.' An odd kind of love, indeed.

'Sure? You're very pale?'

She nodded, though it hurt. Everything hurt.

'I'm sorry, I didn't mean to upset you.' The round face was gentle, understanding. Appallingly so.

'I . . . that's how my husband died, you see. In a plane crash. It was a shock,' she improvised, a transparent half-truth.

'I know, Julie told me,' he said, unembarrassed, and

she was aware that she hadn't fooled him one bit. Was he offering his shoulder to cry on? What had prompted him to draw his bow at the venture? 'A shock for Max, too. People tend to think of Max as being invulnerable—I think he had even come to believe it himself. He lost something in that crash, an ability to *enjoy*. I think he might have found it again, here.'

Sarah looked at him, pain in her heart—for herself and for Max. Perhaps that explained his savagery. She had taunted with weakness and that barb must have sunk far deeper than those he had hooked into her flesh, for she knew their falsity. She shook her head wearily, not really knowing why. If Tom was implying that Max had found it with her . . . but there was no reason for him to think that. Max must flirt with hundreds of women. The pain intensified—she was one of hundreds. No, not even that now!

Tom appeared quite concerned about her lack of colour and Sarah found herself meekly allowing him to shoo her on home. Overwork, he said; the strain of doing two jobs at once. He would square it with Julie.

At home she roamed restlessly around the house, wishing it was possible to go to bed and pull the covers up over her head and summon up those calm, uncomplicated days so recent, yet so far behind her.

She dragged herself into the bathroom and was horrified when she looked in the mirror. A wraith! Dark, burning eyes in a white face. No wonder Tom guessed. Her hot eyes felt dry and sore, her mouth parched, her body feverish, as if pain had absorbed all the moisture from her system.

Maybe it wasn't love, she thought desperately. Maybe it was infatuation, hormonal imbalance—something you could take pills for. All she had to do was hold out until the end of the week, until Max left. Plod on, endure, hide the pain—she was good at doing that. Could she trust Tom? Yes. He understood, he was sorry for her. Curious he might be, but not cruel, not like Max would be if he ever found out. He would laugh, his triumph complete; he would delight in making her suffer. And she would suffer enough without his help. The two things she wanted most in the world right now were the two things he would never give her. His love, and his trust.

CHAPTER ELEVEN

'I DON'T believe this!'

In a luxury suite at the Intercontinental Hotel Sarah confronted a tall, lean, hazel-eyed man over the remains of a luncheon trolley. She was gripped by an uncanny sense of *déjà vu*; this had happened to her before, a little over a month ago. Was the nightmare going to begin all over again?

'You can't—' She stopped, a hand lifting to her heavy head, mesmerised by that familiar expression of hauteur, by the quizzical lift of the brow.

'Can't?' Slowly. Exploring the new word. 'Are there laws in this country of which I am unaware? Are you not a free agent?'

'Of course—I—' Sarah put a hand over her heart. It was beating at an alarming rate. 'But you can't possibly ask me to work for you on the basis of four days' acquaintance! It's not—'

'My dear child,' Sir Richard Wilde looked deeply pained, one thin hand lifting languidly from the arm of his chair, 'if you're going to work for me you must learn to stop thinking in clichéd terms. Originality is my trademark. One must not allow oneself to be hidebound by convention, it stifles creative thinking. It is because I have acted on intuitive decisions that I am where I am today. Would you have me abandon my formula for success now, on your behalf?'

'No . . . no, of course not,' said Sarah hurriedly, still finding the conversation difficult to believe. She had received a casual job offer once before, from a member of the same family—one which, not surprisingly, had never been renewed. She doubted that Sir Richard would deliberately mislead her, but over the past few days she had learned something of his penchant for whimsicality. 'But there is a question of suitability—'

'Ahh.' Shoulders moved expressively under the dark velvet jacket. 'I would never have brought the subject up if I did not think you were suitable,' he said, dismissing the point with his own unique brand of logic. 'And you wear my clothes so well; I knew as soon as I saw your photographs that if we ever met we would be . . . sympathetic.'

He had said as much on his first visit to the *Rags* offices. Sarah, though having had plenty of time to prepare herself, had still been winded by his likeness to Max, and flustered by having her hand kissed instead of shaken.

'You do not have to introduce her,' he had told Julie, who had brought him in from the airport. 'I recognised her at once. But that is not mine,' frowning at Sarah's apricot voile dress, 'and you have lost weight.'

'I'm dieting,' Sarah had lied. She couldn't very well have said, 'I'm pining for your son.'

'It does not suit you,' she was informed, with an exquisite disregard for tact. 'You have height, you need the proportions to match. If you lose any more weight my clothes, which make you look so chic, will be useless to you. An ill-fitting garment is an abomination, do you not think?'

It was skilfully phrased so that in agreeing to the last Sarah was agreeing to the whole. Sir Richard Wilde, she had since discovered, was adept at getting people to agree with him. Not that it made any difference, for if they did not, he ignored them.

'Looking good in your designs is unavoidable,' Sarah pulled herself back to the present, sitting earnestly forward in her chair. 'And it's scarcely a recommendation for a personal assistant.'

'For me it is. You will be constantly at my side; of necessity you must be a discreet advertisement for my talent.'

'But, I have no experience—'

'I should soon give you that. Tell me,' he changed tack

with disarming smoothness, 'are these . . . trivialities an attempt to hide from me the real reason for your refusal?'

'What?' Sarah only just prevented herself from leaping to her feet in shock.

'Do you have a personal dislike of me?' came the bland reply. 'I had the impression that you had enjoyed the last few days, in spite of your reluctance to oblige me. Was I wrong?'

His observance disconcerted her. She had been greatly reluctant, too aware of the poignancy of the situation. Every now and then an intonation, a turn of the head, a phrase would strike a responsive chord and she would be shaken by helpless, hopeless longing. However, she had been given little choice. When Julie had heard that Sir Richard's private secretary had suffered an attack of food poisoning the evening they arrived in Auckland she had immediately offered Jane's services.

'No, no.' Sir Richard had dismissed the possibility with an imperious wave. 'I cannot work with a stranger. Sarah will do—we are already acquainted by proxy. Do you take shorthand?' And when she nodded slowly. 'Good. That is settled.'

A complete autocrat, but a charmer. He had a grass-hopper mind and an uneven temper which he made valiant efforts to control for Sarah's benefit. She was surprised by his thoughtfulness, the small considerations he gave her, and disarmed by his elegant manners. Max had called him a despot, but he was a benevolent despot and not half as formidable as his son had suggested. But then, she thought bitterly, Max's judgements about people had not proved infallible.

Sir Richard was a formidable showman, though. He had been delighted at the stir he had created by deciding to come to New Zealand for the *Images* preview and it had taken little persuasion from Julie to get him to say a few light and witty words at the christening party for the new *Rags & Riches*, held the following day.

Sarah had obediently trailed everywhere after him,

jotting down his constant flow of ideas and memos to himself and to his staff, and watched in awe as he effortlessly extracted every ounce of publicity from his brief visit. Controversial comment and bons mots were scattered in a manner carefully calculated to reach a maximum audience. Sir Richard seemed to positively encourage the pursuit of journalists and photographers.

'Fame, wealth, success—these things I have sought all my life,' he told Sarah confidently. 'In my younger days I struggled against poverty and anonymity in a fiercely competitive field. It took more than just talent to achieve my aims. Why should I now seek to hide from fortune? —that is the action of the weak, the insecure. Privacy —bah! Only what is inside the head and the heart is private, the rest is window-dressing—meant to be seen.'

He spoke, gesturing with passionate intensity—the same intensity with which he approached life. Everything was related to the senses, to feeling, to instinct, to perception. Like now.

'No, you weren't wrong. I like working for you very much . . . you've been very kind.' A faint smile of amusement lit hazel eyes. 'But what about Kevin Matlock?' She had only glimpsed the untidy, bespectacled young man briefly, confined as he was to his hotel bed, but he had looked nice. She would hate to think she was doing him out of his job.

'What about him? You do not imagine that I could function without additional assistance? I have several secretaries, although admittedly I shall be shedding most of them when Max takes over the chairmanship of Wilde's at the end of the month. He will inherit them, or rather disinherit them if I know my son's mania for efficiency.'

Sarah tensed inwardly. Would she never get used to the mention of that name? Thankfully Sir Richard didn't mention him often. She watched warily as the aristocratic figure leaned forward to pour himself another glass of champagne from the chilled bottle on the trolley.

'You seem surprised. Did he not mention his imminent

elevation while he was here?' he continued casually.

'No. Tom did, Tom Forest . . . indirectly,' said Sarah, remembering that momentous conversation in the coffee bar.

'Ah yes, Tom. He gave me a report. He was very impressed with you . . . as I am. I have been thinking along the lines of a personal assistant for some time—it is fate that brings us together, perhaps.'

Lately Sarah had regarded fate with a jaundiced eye.

'What would I be doing, in this job?'

'More or less what you have been doing for the past few days.'

'Oh.' Dare she mention her misgivings? She had no need to, for they were shrewdly analysed.

'Of course, I am limited here. My real work, my only work from now on, is designing, but on a scale which you may yet find difficult to appreciate. I travel the world in search of inspiration, I attend showings, receive clients, visit the factories that make my exclusive fabrics, entertain the rich and famous, all in the cause of fashion. I think you will find your job sufficiently challenging and certainly it will be educational. Why, in ten years' time you may be utilising the valuable experience you have acquired with me in the running of your own fashion empire.'

'As long as I don't aim for yours?' murmured Sarah, half laughingly, then quailed at his expression, fearing she had presumed too much.

'I believe Max has ambitions in that direction.' He smiled, with a brief gleam of maliciousness. 'Though you are quite welcome to fight it out, post-mortem. You might even beat him. Tom told me that you were quite capable of standing up for yourself.'

'But how can you know that I will—' Sarah began, returning to her best defence.

'Know? What is this obsession with knowing?' Sir Richard demanded, white-maned head tilting impatiently. 'I do not know that the designs of my hand will sell, but

I have confidence in my talent. I have confidence in you.'

'But—'

'Please,' he begged, setting down his crystal champagne glass with a frown. 'Do not begin all your sentences
with the word 'but', it begins to grate.'

'I'm sorry, b—I mean, you must know many women
capable of filling the position.'

'Capable, yes, but acceptable? There is a difference. I
receive many requests it is true, but usually those who
seek my employ have an ulterior motive. They wish to get
into modelling, or design, or my bed.' He paused, on that
startling note, giving Sarah a moment to realise that he
was still, though elderly, an attractive man. 'Such motives
inevitably lead to conflicts and I do not need the distraction. I do not want temperament—I have more than
enough of that myself.' It was a relief to discover he had a
sense of humour, that was the first time she had heard him
being remotely humorous about himself. 'I want calmness
and common sense, and intelligence, of course. Most
important, I must have a woman who is not going to burst
into tears every time I shout.'

'And you think I wouldn't?'

Hazel eyes narrowed. 'You have courage, and you are
no sycophant.' He pursed his lips. 'Were you afraid of my
son?'

Sarah swallowed. 'Sometimes.'

'Hmm. He has a devil of a temper when roused.'

'That's what he said about you.'

He acknowledged it. 'But mine blows over as quickly as
it occurs. Max is less flexible. He tries to be logical and life
is not logical. I am logical only by accident.'

'Do . . .? Would . . .?' the burning question was difficult
to phrase, but it had to be asked, even though she intended
to turn down Sir Richard's offer. 'Does your son have
much to do with the Salon?'

'Nothing at all.' Sir Richard clasped his hands over the
ruffled white front of his shirt and smiled with self-
satisfaction. 'I do not permit it. In fact we meet but rarely,

and never socially. Max always was a solitary, secretive boy—' He pulled himself up. 'But we digress. I can see you wish to do some thinking—no!' when she would have protested, 'I insist. You may have until tomorrow to consider your answer. Now, pass me my cane and I will see you to the door.'

Sarah handed over the thin, ivory cane which rested against the trolley, noticing as she did so that Sir Richard seemed to be having some difficulty in rising. Walking across the room with him she could see that the cane wasn't the purely fashionable accessory she had first thought it to be.

'Are you all right, Sir Richard?' she couldn't help asking.

Sir Richard sighed and reached out a hand for hers. Looking down at it she saw he was wearing two rings she had not seen before, gold with some dark stones. They were so heavy that they made the thin white fingers look quite frail.

'Age, I'm afraid, Sarah. I'm no longer a young man. I cannot expect to enjoy the constant good health of my youth. Yet my work drives me on. I cannot afford to show weakness, it is not good press.' He closed his eyes briefly and Sarah was struck by the pallor of his skin. Sir Richard seemed to be so vital, yet even his energy could not be limitless. She remembered the times in the past few days when he had faltered until, conscious of being watched, he had drawn himself up and gone on. Such an active, mentally agile man must fear the encroachments of age, the strictures that it was gradually placing upon him. She felt the stirrings of compassion.

He opened his eyes and smiled, a faintly wistful smile. 'Think well on it, Sarah, and think not only of yourself, but of me too. I need you.'

Stranded in an emotional wilderness, Sarah was tempted. In the past month she had come to the disquieting realisation that she no longer filled her old, comfortable niche at *Rags & Riches*. She had out-grown it and hungered for something more demanding to fill the gaps that had opened in her life. She knew that if it had not been for Max she would have accepted Sir Richard's offer without a single question. But Max was inescapable. What would he say if she turned up under his nose, working for his father? He would think she was chasing him, grovelling for his attention, might even guess the truth. He would have nothing but contempt for her. But so what? He could not despise her any more than he did already and she could not let thoughts of Max rule her life forever, no matter how much she loved him.

How naïve she had been to think that once Max's disturbing physical presence left her shores the tide of her emotions would begin to recede. It was quite the reverse, rolling in like a great wave, gathering strength and momentum, washing away all her feeble attempts to rationalise her love into something less dramatic, less shatteringly painful.

What she had felt like after Simon's death paled by comparison. She had never ached like this . . . the phantom ache of a lost limb; unable to eat properly or sleep, consumed by the effort of keeping his haunting image at bay, so that she might at least *appear* normal. She dreaded the dark, lonely nights, lying awake for hours with her thoughts, but she dreaded even more closing her eyes and falling into that void where her subconscious released all the raw agony and despair that she wouldn't allow herself the luxury of feeling during the day.

Anything would be better than the limbo she was in now, she thought that night as she tossed and turned in the large bed. Even the daily prospect of running into Max, and enduring the kind of cold, empty courtesy he had accorded her during his last week in New Zealand. The scene in the dressing room had obviously been a catharsis for him, so perhaps she was flattering herself to think he would care what she did. Given the relationship between Max and his father, his new responsibilities as Chairman, and the fact that London was a city of millions, the chances of their meeting were really rather slight.

Sarah groaned, burying her face in her pillow, torn by conflicting feelings—wanting to see him again, but afraid of what it would do to her. Max had taught her a harsh lesson about herself. It was true that there was a deep-seated sensuality in her nature, but it was inextricably tied to an equally deep-seated desire for love and commitment. In the final analysis her intellectual need for independence had proved secondary to the feminine desire to seek a mate—yet for Sarah that mate must be one she could respect for being as strong, or stronger than she was.

Simon had tried to dominate her in his fashion, but because he had been basically weak he had not succeeded, and his failure had driven him to intolerable extremes. Max, if he wanted to, could do it effortlessly. He was the kind of man she had thought, in the pseudo-sophistication of her teens, that Simon was. Max had bullied her back into life, into love, and she should be grateful to him for that alone, regardless of the painful consequences. In a few short weeks he had shown her emotional heights and depths she had not been aware existed.

Towards dawn she came to a decision. Love might change—grow or die—but regret was forever. If she didn't take this chance now she would regret it all her life. It was an opportunity to escape the humdrum, to make something of herself, and at the same time perhaps, just perhaps, she might be able to go some way towards healing the breach between Max and herself—regain his respect if not his friendship. Maybe. Perhaps; the stuff dreams are made of.

Sarah stared out the car window at pedestrians quickened by the prospect of another cool April shower, umbrellas unfurling, eyes beginning to turn streetwards, in cynical anticipation of the magical disappearance of every taxi at the first spit of rain. I'm glad I've got mine, she thought, three weeks in London having taught her that a certain amount of selfishness was a necessity if one was to survive in the big city.

Selfishness was also necessary to survive the rigours of her employment. Sarah had found that if she didn't strive to have her needs and opinions acknowledged they were often completely overlooked according to the unwritten law that Sir Richard knew best. Frequently though, he did—as witness the ease with which he detached her from her old life, just as he said he would. In no time at all Sarah found her resignation accepted, notice waived, passage booked with all the red tape in tatters behind her. She was duly farewelled with envious enthusiasm . . . and a whisper in her ear from Julie that if she should ever come across the makings of a good exclusive . . .

When it came to the crunch Sarah had left her job, her home, her country with surprisingly few regrets. Only Roy was a wrench and he was his usual disgustingly cheerful self as she wept over him at the airport.

'Hell, don't ruin my only good T-shirt,' he told her. 'Now go on, cut the apron strings. Be good. Be happy. And if you can't be both at the same time, forget the good!'

'Here you are then, miss.' Sarah realised with a start that the taxi had stopped. She looked out at the multi-storey building shooting up into the darkening sky from a slick, rain-swept pavement.

'Oh, thank you.' She fumbled for change and opened the door, drawing her cream woollen coat tightly around her for the dash to the double-glass doors.

Crossing to the reception desk she glanced around the warm, brightly-lit foyer with interest. This was the first time she had been to Wilde House. Since he had relinquished his chairmanship, Sir Richard no longer had offices here and he actively discouraged his staff making contacts with the wider organisation, in the interests of security. Sarah was more inclined to believe the reasons more personal—Sir Richard, having narrowed down his activities, was jealously guarding the autonomy of his private kingdom. It was true that gossip flowed in torrents through the Wilde Salon, but respect for their monarch's talent and an even healthier respect for his pyrotechnic displays of temper engendered an almost fanatical loyalty amongst Sir Richard's staff—not a whisper escaped their lips outside the Salon walls.

Living-in at Rawlings, Sir Richard's Berkshire home, was one of the conditions of Sarah's employment and she couldn't help but enjoy her sudden ascent into luxury. Work and leisure time tended to become intermingled but at first Sarah was too busy finding her feet and coping with the realisation that her new employer enjoyed better health and a worse temper than he had led her to believe, to find the insularity restrictive. Now, however, she was eager to try her wings.

For three weeks she had done little more than shuttle between Rawlings, where a design team worked under Sir Richard's personal direction, and the Salon in Oxford Street, where the main business was carried out. In either place she was directed to researching records—'learning the ropes'. There would be no trips or social engagements until she was adequately prepared, she was sternly informed, and when she dared to question the value of heavy tomes on the origins of the fashion industry, or etiquette . . .

'There is a purpose in everything I do.' Sir Richard was at his most pompous. 'You are no longer a classless New Zealander, you are part of my entourage and as such I cannot have you embarrassing me with exhibitions of ignorance or ill-breeding. You still have much to learn . . . besides, your new wardrobe has not arrived yet. Those clothes you're wearing—*they are not mine.*' The ultimate condemnation.

Fortunately her custom-made clothes had now arrived, and at last she had been let off the leash. That morning she has been resigned to yet another day 'swotting' in the office at Rawlings while Sir Richard and Kevin Matlock attended an exclusive showing for a very famous client. A phone call after lunch had provided the diversion.

'Sarah, I need you.'

At last. 'Yes, Sir Richard,' she replied meekly.

'Kevin very carelessly omitted to bring some papers that I must study before my evening engagement. You will find them on his desk, in a yellow envelope. Can you bring them to me?'

'Of course. Are you at the Salon?'

'No, I'm at the Duchess' residence in Mayfair, but I don't wish to be interrupted here. I shall be going to the penthouse to change at six, you had best meet me there.'

'The penthouse?' Sarah faltered, clutching the receiver with suddenly slippery fingers.

'Max's place, at Wilde House,' came the impatient reply. 'I often use it when he is away—'

'Away?' A rush of cowardly relief washed over her.

'New York, I understand. For several days. When *I* was chairman I made a point of being in London for at least one week in four; Max makes no such concession . . . I must discuss it with him when he returns.' A pause as he rearranged his thoughts. 'Yes, meet me at six; and wear something formal, the red velvet I think. You may come with me this evening. It is only a small celebration for a minor member of European royalty, but it will be an experience for you—a chance for you to practise the despised etiquette, hmmm?'

Riding up in the small private lift, Sarah watched the lights flick on and off—sixteen, seventeen, eighteen. Her stomach tightened with every floor. Ridiculous to feel scared of an empty apartment, or even of an occupied one. Max was the real reason she was here after all, in spite of all that cleverly contrived mumbo-jumbo about the job being the thing. She hadn't even come close to seeing him, let alone exchanging unpleasantries since she had arrived, but the hopeful fantasies continued to tantalise her. Therein lay the root of her fear—wasn't it better to travel in hope . . .

The lift doors rolled back and she was facing a single, heavy black-padded door across a width of white carpet.

She stepped up and took a deep breath and pushed the lacquered button beside the door. She waited in the thick silence, feeling like a spy. This was Max's home, his lair, and she was here without his knowledge. She felt as guilty as if she was contemplating stealing something.

The door opened with quiet suddenness to reveal a short, middle-aged man in a dark suit. He regarded Sarah with a brief expression of consternation before habitual deference reasserted itself.

'Mrs Carter?' he asked, as if he really wasn't sure, but Sarah had distinctly heard the security guard down below ring the penthouse to check that she was expected.

'Yes. Sir Richard's assistant,' she added unnecessarily, disturbed by the odd vibrations she was receiving.

'Please come in,' he invited, with now impassive politeness. 'My name is Brandon. I'm Mr Wilde's butler.' He took her damp coat as she juggled her handbag and the large envelope of papers. 'If you will come this way.'

Sarah followed the upright figure over the white ceramic tiles of the entry hall, past masses of sub-tropical greenery and into the deep luxurious pile of an electric-blue carpet which covered the floor of the split-level lounge.

On the upper level was a large formal dining area. Steps led down to the lounge proper, acres of it, bounded on one side by floor-to-ceiling windows which looked out over a roof garden with a kidney-shaped pool, calm waters reflecting the dull grey sky.

At first glance Sarah was dazzled by the magnificence of it all. White and a myriad of blues from eggshell to turquoise, rough-textured fabrics contrasted with smooth velvets, glass and steel, ceramics and laminated woods. All the lights were recessed, including the ceiling spots which were directed on to paintings and prints lining the walls. Sculptures from small to life-size were scattered around the room. It was beautiful, but sterile. There were no personal touches, no warmth, no soul.

She turned and caught the butler's black button eyes on

her face and wondered whether her ambivalent opinion showed. Certainly the unspoken question did.

'Wilde Interiors were given a free hand, madam.'

'Oh.' She walked slowly down the steps. If she had Max's money she wouldn't leave the decoration of her home to someone else, she'd have the fun of doing it herself. If she had *Max* she wouldn't care if she lived in a hovel! She pulled herself up sharply. 'Where are the gilded cherubs?' she enquired facetiously, not expecting to be understood.

'Madam has been to Rawlings?'

Sarah looked at the close-cropped head suspiciously. *Madam has.* The butler at Rawlings used the third person too, but never with the hint of dryness she detected in this bland-faced man. And he was actually condescending to engage her in conversation . . . not etiquette at all, and she should know!

'I'm living there at present,' she explained, and with a faint smile. 'I don't think baroque is quite my style.' At least this had an open, uncluttered look, whereas Sir Richard's taste for flourishes had been indulged to the full at Rawlings, with almost claustrophobic results, Sarah thought.

'Indeed, madam.' The black eyes gleamed. 'My tastes are also rather more modern. Would you like a drink while you are waiting for Sir Richard?'

Sarah glanced at her watch. Five-thirty. Sir Richard's timekeeping was at best erratic, prone as he was to distraction, he might arrive in five minutes, or not for another hour.

'That would be nice. A brandy and ginger ale, please.'

She put her bag and envelope down and sat on one of the long white couches that formed an open-ended square by the windows, sinking into the well-padded velvet cushions as Brandon opened a white louvred door in the wall to reveal an extensive array of bottles and glasses. After handing her the amber glass tinkling with ice, he pressed a button concealed in the wall and the raw silk curtains, one shade lighter than the carpet, whispered across the windows. At the same time the ceiling lights dimmed and a collection of small glass spheres heaped on various tables throughout the room began to glow softly.

'How beautiful!' slipped from her involuntarily. 'But I don't see any cords, how do they work?'

'They are operated by microwave. It was Mr Wilde's personal recommendation.'

Here was a chance to ask the question she had been dying to ask, and with as much casualness as she could muster said, 'When is Mr Wilde due back?'

'Due back?' The neutral repetition stopped Sarah's heart in mid-beat.

'Sir Richard told me he was in New York, for several days,' she said quickly, staring at him with wide, dark eyes.

Brandon cleared his throat. 'Ah yes, New York,' he agreed, to Sarah's unutterable relief. His face moved stiffly and she realised that he was actually attempting a smile—butlers would spin in their graves! 'Mr Wilde flies Concorde. It renders the distance so negligible one scarcely considers the United States to be "abroad". I dare say it would take you longer to come down from Berkshire in the rush-hour.'

And with that pleasantry he withdrew, with the request that she call him if she required anything further.

Sarah admonished herself for panicking, it was becoming too much of a habit. She must be cool and composed at all times—how often had Sir Richard drummed that into her? It used to be second nature until Max gatecrashed her life and reduced her to a mass of sensitive nerve-endings. Now she needed it more than ever, now her hopeful travelling was drawing to a close. Damn, her hands were shaking.

Sarah finished her brandy and thought about another, to help calm her nerves. Why not? Max owed her something. A couple of brandies was a bargain price for a broken heart. She got up and found the intercom switch that Brandon had indicated and rang. Brandon delivered without comment and she drank. Better. She was only shaking inside now. Why did she have this awful feeling . . .? Perhaps the apartment was haunted, guarded by Max's unquiet spirit.

She got up and wandered, inspecting herself in the distorted surface of an aluminium sculpture. Lovely dress; pity that the colour held such unfortunate memories. Even though her image was made lopsided by the curving surface of the sculpture, she could see that the deeply-slashed neckline and long, figure-smoothing line of the red velvet suited her. What an angel Sir Richard was! He had designed her hair too—a long braid encircled the back of her head with the rest of her hair cascading in waves from its centre. Regally sexy, he had decreed.

'Regally sexy,' she repeated out loud, feeling less intimidated by the elegant luxury around her. These were the kind of surroundings in which Sir Richard was training her to feel at home. So feel at home she would. She took off her shoes. She put her feet up on the couch, a warm, vibrant splash of colour in the cool room. She didn't even move when she heard the apartment door open and, simultaneously, the phone ring. There was a faint murmur of a voice as Brandon answered the telephone, and the sound of footsteps across the ceramic tiles. Sarah smiled serenely, alcohol warming her veins, waiting for Sir Richard to appear.

CHAPTER TWELVE

'WHAT in the hell are you doing here?'

Sarah blinked at the hostile, brandy-induced apparition at the top of the carpeted stairs.

'Sarah!' The voice was harsh and demandingly savage. In a charcoal-grey suit and tie and white shirt, Max looked formal and remote, every inch a Chairman of the Board. His face was sharper than she remembered, more angles and less flesh; paler too, and the grey strands threading the black sideboards seemed more numerous. But he was still Max, still the man who held her bruised heart in the hollow of his uncaring hand.

Paralysed by the shock of his sudden appearance Sarah could only stare and wait as he set down his briefcase and came slowly, frowningly down the steps and across the room towards her.

'Sarah?' The husky question came as Max narrowed his eyes and half raised a hand from his side as if to touch her, as if he doubted the evidence of his senses.

'Max . . .?' was all her poor vocal chords could manage, but it was enough. His hand dropped and he took an audible breath.

'You seem as surprised as I am,' he said, after a moment. 'Yet why should you be? You must have come here to see me.'

He undid the buttons of his jacket, not taking his eyes of the sudden flush on Sarah's face. He shrugged it off and sat down on the couch opposite, stretching out his long legs, hands splayed tautly over his muscled thighs. He looked her over and the ghost of a smile touched the hard mouth.

'You look very much at home.'

The faint sarcasm thawed Sarah's frozen limbs. She hurriedly swung her legs off the couch, sitting up to search for her red shoes with her feet.

'Did I say I objected?'

'I . . .' Sarah stopped, confused by the hint of humour. He had been unmistakably angry when he had walked in and seen her there. Why was he now looking as though . . . as though . . . 'I thought you were in New York.'

'I was; until this morning. Now I'm here. And you're here too. And you still haven't told me why.' He was mocking her, but gently, and it completely shattered her composure—it was so unexpected . . . so *impossible*. That he should smile, like that, at her, after all that had passed between them.

'I—I've brought some papers,' she said vaguely, eyes going hungrily over the lounging body, storing up the memory of his nearness.

'You came all this way just to bring me some papers? How kind of you, Sarah. But couldn't you have posted them?'

He didn't even ask to see them, didn't even really seem interested, he just stared at her with that disturbing smile.

'They're not for you.'

'Not for me?'

'Your—Sir Richard asked me to—'

'My father!' It was as though she had slapped him, the smile vanished in an instant, his face hardening with suspicion as he stood up. Sarah stood up too and was dismayed to find that without her shoes she only came up to his shoulder. 'What has my father to do with it?' Suddenly something else registered with him. 'And where did you get that dress, it's from the Wilde Spring Collection? What's going on?'

'You don't know?' breathed Sarah, one hand coming up to cover her horrified mouth. 'I thought you knew. I spoke to Tom on the phone last week. He knew. I thought you knew, too.' She had been unsure what to think, whether to be relieved that Max had made no effort to jeopardise her new job or depressed that he obviously didn't give a damn. But if he hadn't known . . .

'Knew what?' articulated Max dangerously, and Sarah shivered wordlessly. 'So help me, Sarah, if you don't stop stalling and tell me, I swear I'll—' He had actually slipped rigid hands around her slender neck when they were interrupted.

'Excuse me, sir.' Brandon showed no surprise at finding his master on the verge of strangling a female visitor. Perhaps he was used to such strange scenes, thought Sarah a trifle hysterically, before she realised she was being addressed.

'That was Sir Richard on the telephone, Mrs Carter. He apologises for the delay. He has been held up at the Salon, but he still wants you to wait. He had a message for you, too, sir,' he addressed the ominously quiet Max. 'He asked me to convey his best wishes. He said you would understand.'

'What?' The uncomfortable grip on Sarah's throat dropped away as hazel eyes glared at the bland-faced butler. Seconds ticked away before Max said softly, through his teeth, 'Get out.'

'Will you be wanting—?'

'Get out!' Max bawled and with remarkable calm Brandon bowed to Sarah and withdrew, managing to exude dignity through every retreating pore.

'Now . . .' Eyes that held a brilliant glitter were turned back on Sarah. She drew on the remains of her Dutch courage.

'I work for him.'

'Work for whom?' said Max blankly. Obviously never in his worst dreams had it occurred to him . . .

'Sir Richard,' she whispered. 'I'm his personal assistant.'

He looked incredulous, furious. 'When? How?' he shot at her.

He offered me the job when he came out to New Zealand,' said Sarah, endeavouring to conquer a sudden queasiness. 'I've been working for him virtually ever since.'

'You're living here?'

'A—at Rawlings.'

A red flush covered Max's cheekbones and he gave her a look of baffled anger. 'My father doesn't need another personal assistant, and you damned well know it!'

Sarah's chin lifted proudly. 'He says he does.'

'I'll bet he does, and I bet you weren't hard to convince.' Max drew his lips back from his teeth, but it was more a snarl then a smile. 'You must have been glad you lost your chance with me. My father is much richer and not likely to be as *demanding* as a younger man.'

It was clear what he meant and the insult rendered Sarah icily sober. 'You're insane—can you hear yourself?' she said in a cold little voice. 'If you have no respect for me, you should at least have some for your father. He—'

'Oh, for God's sake shut up!' Max ground out rudely and went over to the bar. 'I don't need your lectures.' He didn't come back with his drink but prowled about beyond the square of the couches. Sarah found her shoes and put them on, feeling shattered. This was it. The end of the journey. And nothing had changed. She watched his restless pacing helplessly. He moved fluidly, like the big cats at the zoo, back and forth, a resentful captive. Eventually he stopped and glared at her sullenly.

'And you can stop looking at me like that, damn you. You know I didn't mean it.' He thrust an impatient hand through thick black hair. He sounded for all the world like a sulky boy who knows he has done wrong but doesn't want to admit it. In spite of the sheer awfulness of the situation Sarah felt a dull flicker of amusement.

'I'm glad I amuse you!' The growl wiped the smile off her face and she snapped back:

'Well, it's laughable. He's old enough to be my grandfather and most of the time he treats me like a recalcitrant child. We're only going out tonight because he's finally decided he can trust me not to eat peas off my knife.' For an instant she thought Max was going to smile but he was still simmering.

'All right, I get the message. I've already apologised. Should I go down on my knees?'

A glorious surge of righteous indignation freed Sarah from the last bonds of nervousness. To hell with the surly brute! Had she actually imagined that she loved the moody devil?

'Only if it'll improve your temper! You were right about you and your father being alike in some ways. You both sulk if you don't get things exactly your own way. I should be used to it by now.'

Max hunched his shoulders and stared at her with thinly veiled dislike. Some of the drink slopped out of his glass as he moved. He swore softly and rubbed at the mark with a careless shoe then refilled his glass before coming over to sprawl opposite her again, asking with a restrained belligerence:

'Why do you work for him then? I seem to recall you once shuddered at the very idea.'

'I didn't say I don't like working for him. Actually he's been very kind.' Since Max made no move to reply, unpleasantly or otherwise, Sarah plugged on, making polite conversation to a stranger. When she mentioned, in passing, that this was her first expedition on her own Max roused himself to interruption.

'That doesn't sound like you. I thought you didn't like to be caged, in any sense.'

Sarah shrugged. She was not about to confess to the slightest tinge of frustration. 'Sir Richard said my rough edges needed polishing. And they did. I feel much more confident now, quite equal to anything he might throw at me.'

'Knowing my father, that could be termed literally. I take it then, that he requested you work for him and not vice versa.'

'I couldn't believe it at first.' She explained briefly about Kevin Matlock's illness and the circumstances

surrounding Sir Richard's surprising offer, warily eyeing
the now expressionless face opposite. Max seemed to have
calmed down but his stillness could conceal anything.

'So here you are—polished and perfumed to perfec-
tion,' he murmured at last. 'Tell me, why did you think I
was still in New York?'

'Your father said you were,' Sarah replied, thankful
that they were at last communicating normally. 'And
Brandon—' Black eyebrows flew up as Sarah en-
deavoured to remember just what his butler had said.
'Well, he didn't actually *say* you were still there, but
he . . .'

'Implied it. How well I know Brandon's implications,'
drily and then, almost under his breath. 'Damn him for
his interference! My father can resist everything but the
temptation to organise the world to his own dramatic
satisfaction.'

'He really does need an assistant,' Sarah insisted loyal-
ly. 'He told me himself that his health—'

A short amused laugh greeted this bit of naïvety and
Max gulped half his drink without enjoyment before
saying, savagely: 'I don't like being manipulated.'

'*You* do it all the time,' Sarah pointed out, beginning to
think that all this moody, broody behaviour had nothing
to do with her at all. His anger seemed more directed at his
father than at her, and she was just the convenient
whipping boy. 'Anyway, now that you're chairman I
don't see how your father can manipulate you.'

'Don't you? My God, you're a dumb little cow sometimes.'

Sarah stiffened at the casually uttered insult.

'Intelligent enought to be damned good at my job.'

'Intelligent, but dumb,' agreed Max infuriatingly.

'I don't know what you're talking about.'

'That's what I mean.' Her irritation seemed to have
restored his good humour. 'If I thought you *did*, you'd
have been on the doorstep by now. And you didn't land
the job, the job landed you . . . well and truly.' He laid his

head back against the cushions and studied her through thick, dark lashes. 'You look thinner.'

'So do you,' countered Sarah nervously. He had always been unpredictable, but never this much—blowing hot and cold with one breath. 'You look tired, too.' The blue shadows were back around his eyes, the bones of his temples more pronounced, giving him a lean and hungry look.

'I am.' The admission surprised her. The Max she knew would have denied it. 'Have you been homesick?'

'I haven't had time. In any case, there wasn't a lot to feel homesick for.' *Only you, only you.*

'What about lover-boy?'

'If you mean Roy Merrill,' said Sarah, in a carefully neutral voice, 'he was very pleased for me. And he was never my lover.'

They measured glances for a few seconds, and Max was the first to look away. 'Well, it doesn't matter now.' The flat voice hammered a shaft of steel through her heart.

'No.'

Suddenly the effort of sitting there, trying to appear unmoved, was too much. She got up and walked restlessly, as the man had done before her, revealing her agitation more with each passing minute. She wished she had never come. She wished she was sophisticated enough to smile and mean it. She wished the polish was diamond-hard and not just skin deep. She forced herself to display an interest in the various works of art, though in reality she saw nothing, too acutely aware of the dark man watching her every move. She had never known such silence, like the end of the world, and the longer it grew the more impossible it was to break. She almost jumped out of her skin when, on consulting her watch for the tenth time in as many minutes a velvety voice floated in from the edges of eternity.

'You may as well relax, Sarah, you're in for a very long wait.'

'What?' She gave him a hunted glance.

'We may as well make ourselves comfortable . . . find a pleasant way to pass the time. Come over here.'

Sarah's skin prickled as she registered that certain lilt. 'What for?'

He smiled lazily and her eyes widened. Surely he wouldn't have the gall to . . .

'Come here and see.' *He would*.

'No,' she said, violently, staying where she was, a safe distance of several metres. Even so she took a hasty step back as Max rose slowly to his feet, yawning and stretching until the long body shuddered, every muscle seeming to settle back into complete relaxation. He no longer looked tired, but somehow refreshed, his smile widening as if her increasing nervousness amused him, pleased him.

'You always were nervy around me,' he observed. 'Some things don't change, do they, Sarah?'

Sarah licked her lips and his eyes dropped to her mouth. 'Like that. You always do it when you're scared; and I always find it erotic.' He paused and the blood thundered in Sarah's ears. She was convinced that either she was drunk, or he was, or they both were. 'Are you scared of me now, Sarah?'

'Should I be?' She meant it to be discouraging but it came out a squeak.

'Yes. Oh, yes.' He came towards her on catlike tread and she backed away.

'Max, stop it!'

'Stop what?' he asked innocently, still coming.

'This stupid game, whatever it is.'

'No game, Sarah,' he said, grinning wolfishly as she backed up against a large white stone sculpture, hemmed in by the back of the couch on one side and a table topped with the glowing globes on the other. I've had enough of games. This time it's for real.'

Sarah's nerves were as taut as wire as she watched him stop an arm's-length away, resting a lean hip against the back of the couch, casually unbuttoning and removing his waistcoat, and undoing several of his shirt buttons. Butterflies began a frantic dance in Sarah's stomach. She craved his touch, his soft words, but not like this. He thought she was an easy lay, a body with which to relieve the frustrations of a tiring day.

'Your father will be here any minute,' she said desperately, but Max was ignoring her flutterings, his mouth twitching as he looked at her.

'How clever of you to wear red, it's so . . . evocative. I remember the last time you wore a red dress. All I could think of was what was underneath it—the honey-flavoured skin, those little shreds of lace . . . kissing you up against that wall, arousing you until all you could do was moan for me. Remember?' His voice had dropped to a husky murmur, his eyes almost clouded as he watched the rapid rise and fall of her breasts. Sarah almost moaned then. She remembered. Every inch of her body tingled with the memory.

'I see you do,' he said dreamily and she, struggling weakly in the silken web of sensuality, only gave him token resistance when he pounced, pulling her towards him until their bodies bumped together.

'That's better. Little fool, stop fighting me. This is what you're here for.'

With one arm around her he thrust his other hand into her hair and tilted her head back kissing her roughly. It was as though he had never stopped.

Still holding her he let himself fall over the low back of the couch, carrying her with him so that she lay on his chest, hair falling in a silky curtain around their faces. His mouth moved against hers hot and hungry, parting her lips with an eager tongue. It happened so suddenly, that much-desired, long dreamed-of embrace, that Sarah was instantly excited—pride, scruples melting like sugar in the mouth. He was rough, but it was a roughness born of passion, not anger, and Sarah welcomed it, welcomed also the change of that first devouring assault to a mutual exploration.

She closed her eyes, sighing as his mouth moved over

her delicate ear, moving her own mouth against the warm muskiness of his neck, loving the feel of domination it gave her to lie on top of him, to feel his body tremble beneath hers.

His hands moved through the warm softness of her hair and he used it to pull her sideways and roll with her so that now he was lying half on top of her, his thighs heavy on hers, hands moving over her as he kissed her face, her throat and the upper curve of her breasts above the dress. She twisted, pressing herself feverishly closer to him, hair spilling in a cascading wave over the side of the couch to the floor.

She felt the warmth of his hand on her leg, sliding up the heavy velvet of her dress, stroking her thigh with soft, circular movements and felt his slurred murmur against her throat.

'How I've waited for his . . . moan for me, sweet vixen, like you did before . . .'

His hand moved up under her dress, sliding across her satiny stomach as he brushed his mouth back and forth across her skin just above the deep curve of her bodice. The fabric suddenly felt tight and constrictive, heavily encasing her, inhibiting her enjoyment. The blood rushed dizzily to her head as it drooped over the side of the couch. A physical sensation that was close to swooning, a voluptuous sighing, straining sensation took hold of her. She was gasping for air in his arms, dying of sweetness and love . . .

Next moment she was being shaken out of her daze, the caressing hands had become a vice about her waist.

'What did you just say?'

'Hmmm?' She didn't care, she tried to pull his head back down but he wouldn't let her. He dragged her so that they were both sitting up.

'What did you say?'

'I don't know . . . I don't remember,' she said, frightened. She didn't want to think, or talk, she wanted to make love. She no longer cared how little he thought of her, she wanted one beautiful, intimate memory to take away with her. To sustain her against the bitter truth she had faced tonight.

'Something about loving me.'

'No.' Not even in the incandescent heat of the moment could she have betrayed herself so utterly. 'No, I said —make love to me.'

'You lying bitch, you said you loved me!' He shook her brutally hard and she choked back a sob. Was he angry because he thought she had said it as a form of black-mail to try and worm her way back into his good books?

'You must have misheard me—'

The hell I did!' He put a hand on the side of her face and forced it back as she would have looked away from him. ' "I love you", you said—and you meant it. That's why you took that job with my father, because you wanted to get close to *me*: because you were desperate enough to settle for whatever you could get—isn't it? *Isn't it?*' His eyes burned yellowly into hers and she knew by his look, his grip, that he was intent on forcing an answer. God, how he must hate her, to do this to her!

'Perhaps I did say it,' she said wildly, giving him the lesser victory, 'but you already know how responsive I am to you physically. You can make me say anything, do anything, when I'm in your arms—'

'And have done so . . . but not tonight. I wasn't asking anything of you tonight. I wasn't taking advantage of your sexual thrall,' he gave a peculiar, excited laugh. 'What you said you said of your own free will. And you'll say it again.'

'No!' With an anguished cry she tore herself out of his hands and fled, plunging through the nearest door, down a short hallway into the dimness beyond. A dead end; she turned at bay.

'You're always trying to get away from me, darling,' came the silky drawl from the dark silhouette in the doorway. 'Haven't you learned yet how hopeless it is?' He couldn't know how true that was. 'This time you've made a truly Freudian slip.'

The room leaped into life as he touched a switch by his side and Sarah realised with dismay that she was in a bedroom—his bedroom. It had to be. All white and black and silver, the tubular chrome curves of the bedstead rising flatly from the wide, wide, black fur-covered bed.

Sarah could feel herself beginning to shake, beginning to weaken. What did pride matter? He was right, she would settle for whatever she could get . . .

'Max . . . your father . . .' she panted, a last fatalistic attempt to put him off the scent.

'My father, my sweet little innocent, won't be coming to the party.'

'What?' Distractedly she stared at him.

'Didn't I say you were dumb?' He didn't move from the doorway, just looking, savouring her nervous fear. 'He set you up, and me. We may as well go along with it. Did you know it was my birthday today?'

Sarah stared at the madman. Did he want her to sing 'Happy Birthday'?

'He likes his presents to be unique, extravagant . . . and superbly wrapped . . .' She didn't need his eyes wandering over her to tell her what he meant.

'You're mad,' she breathed.

'Insane,' he agreed. 'You told me that before. And my father told me, when I spoke to him on the telephone this morning that when I got back from New York, he had a present for me that he would deliver tonight.' His eyelids drooped. 'And that it was something I wanted . . . very . . . much.'

'He wouldn't.' Sarah whispered, feeling used, confused.

'He did. It's the kind of devious game he likes to play.' Max smiled, too kindly. 'I imagine you're feeling now like I felt when I found out you worked for him. You'll get used to it, and him.'

'But how, why should he?' Sarah's fear had receded on

impact of this new bombshell, as she slowly fathomed the implications.

'No doubt he was concerned about my mental health. My convalescence in New Zealand didn't seem to have had the effect he was hoping for—so he obviously did some detective work. And if Tom knew you were here, I can guess where he got his best information from.'

Oh, God—Tom! What sort of information had he provided Sir Richard with? His suspicion that she loved Max? No wonder Sir Richard had been so smug when she accepted his job, and all the time he had been planning this—coolly working it all to a precise timetable. And all because . . . her eyes stopped looking inward and re-focussed on the man who had moved into the room without her realising it and now stood an arm's-length away, watching the expressions chase across her face. Watching her reach the unbelievable conclusion.

'Why should he think you wanted me?' she asked, hardly daring to voice the question out loud.

'Perhaps he came here snooping.' His steady gaze went past her. 'And saw that.'

Numb as her brain was, she knew what she would see before she turned. Knew, feared, hoped. And there it was. On the wall, by the bed, displayed by the soft lighting. The picture, Roy's picture—that alluring, inviting Sarah —safe in some rich American's private collection, so she'd thought. She closed her eyes, and opened them. It was still there, telling her something, and she was terrified of misunderstanding the message.

She turned back, skin milk-white, eyes huge and dark.

'Why?'

'You know why.'

But she didn't. She couldn't make the step, the leap from fantasy to fantastic reality.

'Tell me.'

He moved to touch her and stopped, warned by her expression. 'Did you mean it when you said you loved me?'

She knew what he wanted. He wanted her to make it easy for him. But he had hurt her too much. Let him risk rejection, know the pain of uncertainty.

'Tell me.'

He began stiffly, guardedly. 'I knew it was going to be sold in America so I had my dealer put up a standing bid for any new works of Merrill's that came on the market. I got it two weeks ago.' His voice became rough, and he wouldn't look at her, staring instead at his fingers playing lightly over the chrome of the bed end. 'I didn't have you, so I had to have the next best thing, no matter what it cost me. And it cost me quite a lot.' The smile was a mere twitch. 'I flew it out first-class Concorde on a seat all of its own, with an escort.'

'You wanted it that much?'

He looked at her, dark lashes flickering, sweat breaking out on his forehead as though this was a labour of physical strength. 'I wanted *you* that much. It didn't start out that way. In the beginning I just wanted to go to bed with you, to draw out the fire that I sensed inside you, for my own pleasure. Yet the more I got to know you the more I wanted to know. You tried to be so dull . . . but with me you were sharp and fierce and passionate, and you had an inner strength and intelligence that I liked. And then, and then—' he broke off and swallowed, and his voice became thick with effort as he forced himself to continue.

'That night at your place the whole world crashed in on me. I felt humiliated, betrayed, as if I had some moral claim on you when in fact I had none. I felt angry, jealous, things I've never felt before about a woman. I didn't know what was happening to me and I hated feeling so . . . so helpless before you.'

The bewilderment was there on his face and in his voice, as he had felt it then. He was carrying on an internal struggle, grimly intent on stripping away a lifetime's defences—on holding up each imperfection to the light for her inspection.

'The next day, when you told me about your relationship with Merrill I wanted to believe you so badly that it scared me. I wouldn't let myself listen. For the first time I was in an emotional situation I couldn't control. It was important that you be a cheat and a liar and a promiscuous tart, because that gave me the perfect excuse to reject you, to regain control. But it didn't work like that. I still wanted you, and I hated myself for it so I—I—*God*!' He closed his eyes briefly, clinging tightly to the cold chrome and sucking in a painful breath. 'When I think what I did, what I said . . . I thought you must know and be laughing at me for my weakness.'

He jerked his head sideways, but not before Sarah had seen the strange glitter in his eyes and was awed. Tears . . . for her . . . and bitter self-condemnation. Suddenly she didn't want to hear any more of this forced confession. She didn't want to hurt as she had been hurt, she wanted to protect him, to enfold him in her love, never to demand but to give and give without counting cost.

She reached out and put her arms around him tightly, resisting his attempt to detach her. She laid her head against the slightly damp skin of his chest, feeling the soft body-hair tickling her cheek, hearing the erratic beat of his heart.

'No more,' she begged softly. 'You don't have to explain anything to me, Max . . . I understand.'

He pulled her head up, cupping her face with gentle hands. 'I hurt you. I owe you this. I can only hope you will forgive me. I came raging back here like a wounded tiger; no wonder my father and Tom decided that drastic measures were called for. I realised, you see, as soon as I left, that I had bungled my chance of real happiness. That like a blind fool I had run away from the very thing I'd been seeking all my life, and given up hope of ever finding.'

He groaned and Sarah was amazed that he couldn't see what was in her face. She knew now what he meant about Roy not mattering, the past only mattered in the sense that it had brought them here, together, in the present.

Couldn't he see that she no longer wanted, or needed to receive his complete submission?

'I love you,' she said softly. Then with force and passion: 'I love you and I'll say it, in your arms and out, for as long as you want me to. I'm yours for as long as you want me.'

He looked white, shaken, so that she smiled and said:

'You knew.' And he smiled too, rather crookedly.

'Wishing made it so.' His voice took on a tone of wonder that caressed Sarah with warmth. 'I never thought I'd fall in love. Take a wife, have children eventually, yes—if only to placate my father. But love? It's a strange country, I don't know it, I don't know the language—'

Sarah laid a small, soft hand over his mouth, feeling joyous, generous—

'I'll teach you. But as long as you feel it you don't have to say it.'

She felt his warm breath against her palm.

'Oh, but I want to. I want to be very explicit.' The smile faded and his voice took on a deep, new strength. 'I love you, Sarah. You're the only woman I've ever said that to. First love, last love, my love.' He kissed her to punctuate the phrases, and the kisses grew slower, longer, as they swayed together, locked in each other's arms, affirming the vow.

'No more objections to being set up?' Sarah enquired huskily at length, as Max nuzzled the long, lovely curve of her throat.

He lifted his head and grinned. It took light years off the charcoal-suited chairman. 'You know why I was so furious? I had my own plans and I saw them go up in smoke before my eyes. Come and see.'

He led her over to the bedside table and sat her, very properly, on the edge of the bed while he drew out a small, rectangular case. He placed it in her hands and sat beside her to watch her open it.

Sarah found the hidden catch and gasped at the sight of an exquisitely wrought brooch, a golden fox with flashing, ruby eyes and lolling tongue, surrounding by an inter-twining of chased gold vines. There were two tiny earrings to match, each a copy of the fox's head.

'For me?' she breathed and Max smiled tenderly at her disbelief.

'I have airline tickets too. I intended to come out and prostrate myself. To woo you properly,' he said softly with wry self-mockery. 'I had them specially made to my own design. I made myself wait until they were finished, hoping that the breathing space would give you time to stop hating me for the things I did to you.'

'They're beautiful.' Sarah touched the delicate jewel-lery with a shaking hand. 'Nobody's ever given me any-thing so beautiful.'

'And unique, like you,' Max said, immensely satisfied by her words. 'And this, too . . .'

No box this time. A ring—aflame with rubies, afire with diamonds.

'Put it on. No, this hand,' taking it from her nerveless fingers. 'To celebrate what I hope will be the shortest engagement in history.'

'Engagement?' Sarah thought she was going to faint, the jewellery forgotten. 'You want to *marry* me?'

'Of course I want to marry you,' he said violently. 'What do you think I've been saying? That I love you and want you to be my mistress.' Her face gave her away. 'You must have a very low opinion of me! I suppose I can't blame you for that.'

'No.' Sarah laid her hand on his arm, felt the rigidity of his muscles and hastened to reassure him. 'I only meant that I never thought . . . I mean . . .' she floundered, knowing it would hurt him if she told the truth, that she hadn't thought his love sufficiently strong for him to give up his celebrated freedom for it.

'God, is it marriage that's the problem?' he said sud-denly, a raw note of uncertainty in his voice. 'Has your experience with Simon put you off?' The emotional strug-gle showed on his face as he said, slowly, 'I don't want a so-called "open marriage", but if you'd feel trapped with anything more conventional—' he broke off, wounded by her laughter at this most serious of moments. 'What are you laughing about?'

'You. So abject.' Sarah could hardly speak for giggles, he was so far *wrong*. 'I'm enjoying it while I can, once we're married I suppose you'll be your usual arrogant self again.'

His eyes gleamed with a return of masculine confidence. 'You can't refuse me now, darling, my father would never forgive you.'

Sarah sobered. 'But he didn't know you wanted to marry me. Will he . . . approve, do you think?'

It was Max's turn to laugh. He slid an arm around her velvet waist and hugged her against his hard body. 'Approve. Darling, you've been signed, sealed and delivered by his own fair hands. You've domesticated the tiger, of course he approves.'

'Hmm, I always was good with wild animals,' Sarah murmured, tremors beginning to build up in her body as the strong, sensitive hands began to wander.

'Don't distract me,' came the order. 'I'm unwrapping my birthday present.'

Before she realised what had happened Sarah was flat on her back on the bed, being ruthlessly kissed. With practised economy of movement Max neatly extracted her from her dress, so obviously eager that her mischievous streak was awakened. Secure in his love, she pushed him away, wide-eyed when he slid his hands over her lacy red bra.

'No, Max, not until we're married, it wouldn't be right.'

He looked stunned. 'You want to wait? It'll be at least three days before—' he choked to a stop as Sarah's eyes began to dance.

'Vixen,' he growled, threateningly. 'For that bit of heresy I shall make love to you until you beg for mercy.'

'Try and make me,' she teased provocatively, enticing him with her lace-clad body, and trying half-heartedly to escape as he lunged for her.

They wrestled playfully until it was no longer play, until desire caught up with them, overtook them, and the rhythms of love established themselves in soft, sighing sounds.

Sarah gave herself with delight, with love and uninhibited joy and was rewarded with unimaginable pleasure when he finally took her, with infinite skill and a kind of gentle savagery that carried her with him to the far peaks, breathing as one the thin, rarified air of ecstasy, sharing a passion that was pure and white and blindingly fierce.

And afterwards when he held her trembling body against his, and licked the sweet salt tears from her cheeks, she knew at last the peace of utter contentment. That this love she had found was not a trap, but a door to a new, exciting and enriching life.

Author **JOCELYN HALEY,**
also known by her fans as **SANDRA FIELD**
and **JAN MACLEAN,** now presents her
eighteenth compelling novel.

DREAM of DARKNESS

With the help of the enigmatic Bryce Sanderson,
Kate MacIntyre begins her search for the meaning behind
the nightmare that has haunted her since childhood.
Together they will unlock the past and forge a future.

**Available at your favorite
retail outlet in NOVEMBER.**

You're invited to accept 4 books and a surprise gift Free!

Acceptance Card

Mail to: Harlequin Reader Service®

In the U.S.	In Canada
2504 West Southern Ave.	P.O. Box 2800, Postal Station A
Tempe, AZ 85282	5170 Yonge Street
	Willowdale, Ontario M2N 6J3

YES! Please send me 4 free Harlequin Romance® novels and my free surprise gift. Then send me 6 brand new novels every month as they come off the presses. Bill me at the low price of $1.65 each ($1.75 in Canada)—an 11% saving off the retail price. There are no shipping, handling or other hidden costs. There is no minimum number of books I must purchase. I can always return a shipment and cancel at any time. Even if I never buy another book from Harlequin, the 4 free novels and the surprise gift are mine to keep forever.

116 BPR-BPGE

Name	(PLEASE PRINT)

Address	Apt. No.

City	State/Prov.	Zip/Postal Code

This offer is limited to one order per household and not valid to present subscribers. Price is subject to change.

ACR-SUB-1

Experience the warmth of ...

Harlequin Romance

**The original romance novels.
Best-sellers for more than 30 years.**

Delightful and intriguing love stories
by the world's foremost writers
of romance fiction.

Be whisked away to dazzling
international capitals ...
or quaint European villages.
Experience the joys of falling in love ...
for the first time, the best time!

Harlequin Romance

**A uniquely absorbing journey
into a world of superb romance reading.**

**No one touches the heart of a woman
quite like Harlequin!**

R-111

You're invited to accept 4 books and a surprise gift Free!

Acceptance Card

Mail to: **Harlequin Reader Service®**

In the U.S.
2504 West Southern Ave.
Tempe, AZ 85282

In Canada
P.O. Box 2800, Postal Station A
5170 Yonge Street
Willowdale, Ontario M2N 6J3

YES! Please send me 4 free Harlequin Presents® novels and my free surprise gift. Then send me 8 brand new novels every month as they come off the presses. Bill me at the low price of $1.75 each ($1.95 in Canada) — an 11% saving off the retail price. There are no shipping, handling or other hidden costs. There is no minimum number of books I must purchase. I can always return a shipment and cancel at any time. Even if I never buy another book from Harlequin, the 4 free novels and the surprise gift are mine to keep forever.

108 BPP-BPGE

Name _____ (PLEASE PRINT)

Address _____ Apt. No. _____

City _____ State/Prov. _____ Zip/Postal Code _____

This offer is limited to one order per household and not valid to present subscribers. Price is subject to change.

ACP-SUB-1